"I'm not what you want."

"But you could be," Kate murmured.

Jay took a step closer and Kate found herself leaning in to him, the general warmth she'd felt earlier building.

"This doesn't make sense. We're adversaries. Yet around you I get this crazy impulse—"

"I feel it, too." She lifted her head, studying the depth of his blue eyes.

His hand moved to the small of her back. And then they were kissing. Lips on lips, tender and sweet.

When they separated, she dropped her forehead to his chest. The depth of her longing was so deep she could hardly breathe. "Tell me this isn't crazy? Do we really want this?"

Dear Reader,

Imagine you're single, thirty-something, living in New York City. (Perhaps some of you are!) So many people all around you. But how do you find that one special someone with whom you're meant to spend your life, and possibly raise a family? Ironically, it seems that when we're most focused on other aspects of our lives, that's when cupid's arrow strikes.

This is what happens to the hero and heroine in this book. Kate Cooper has ended a relationship with her fiancé after finding out he cheated on her. The last thing she wants is another man in her life. Jay Savage is reeling from his sister's recent death and adjusting to his new role as guardian to her son. There has never been a less perfect time to fall in love.

And yet...guess what...that's exactly what's about to happen as they compete for a single job opening at the Fox & Fisher Detective Agency.

I hope you enjoy their story and that you look for the final book of the series, *Receptionist Under Cover,* available next month. I'm always happy to hear from readers so please send me an e-mail sometime and let me know how you're doing. Also, do check my Web site, www.cjcarmichael.com, regularly for news about my books and to enter my "Surprise!" contests.

Happy reading!

C.J. Carmichael

TM B

The P.I. Contest
C.J. Carmichael

TORONTO • NEW YORK • LONDON
AMSTERDAM • PARIS • SYDNEY • HAMBURG
STOCKHOLM • ATHENS • TOKYO • MILAN • MADRID
PRAGUE • WARSAW • BUDAPEST • AUCKLAND

Recycling programs
for this product may
not exist in your area.

ISBN-13: 978-0-373-71617-3

THE P.I. CONTEST

Copyright © 2010 by Carla Daum.

www.eHarlequin.com

Printed in U.S.A.

ABOUT THE AUTHOR

Hard to imagine a more glamorous life than being an accountant, isn't it? Still, C.J. Carmichael gave up the thrills of income tax forms and double-entry bookkeeping when she sold her first book in 1998. She has now written more than twenty-eight novels for Harlequin Books, and invites you to learn more about her books, see photos of her hiking exploits, and enter her surprise contests at www.cjcarmichael.com.

Books by C.J. Carmichael

With love to all my friends who celebrated the milestone birthday with me this year:

Simon, Myrna, Rhonda, Susan, Fred, Shannon, Kate, Wendy, Lynda, Lorna, Myrna-Joy, Debbie, Cheryl, Dennis. And Voula…your turn is coming soon!

Cripes, but we're getting old!

CHAPTER ONE

Kᴀᴛᴇ Cᴏᴏᴘᴇʀ ᴛᴡɪsᴛᴇᴅ ᴛʜᴇ engagement ring on her finger, slowly working it over her knuckle, then into her palm. As a cop with the NYPD, she understood that the most illuminating evidence often came from the most innocuous of sources.

She hadn't expected this to apply to her personal life, though.

"Hey, Kate." Max Beranger tapped her shoulder. "Can I borrow a pen?" He tossed his into the trash with disgust.

Max had been her patrol partner tonight. Now they were filling out their end-of-shift reports. Absentmindedly, she handed him one of the pens she normally hoarded, her mind still on the conversation she'd had with her neighbor earlier in the evening, on her way to work.

"Thanks," Max said.

"Sure." Janet Beaker lived in the apartment across the hall from her and Conner. Janet was single, well-educated and active—she had a life of her own and no need to live vicariously through other people's dramas.

Which was one reason Kate was inclined to believe her. The other reason was her own gut reaction to what

Janet had to say. *Yes,* she'd thought. *Damn it, yes. I knew something was wrong.*

Because there had been signs…such as coming home dead tired after a long night shift to find freshly laundered sheets on the bed and fresh towels in the bathroom.

She'd thought, great, Conner was finally pulling his share in the housekeeping department.

After six months of living together, she should have known better.

"You've been quiet tonight," Max said. "What's up?"

"Nothing." Officers had begun arriving for the 7:00 a.m. shift. Slowly men and women filtered into the room, and she dismissed each face until she saw the man she'd been waiting for—Conner Lowery. Just twelve hours ago she'd thought she was going to marry him, have babies with him, love him forever.

Now the sight of him brought a spasm of pain to her empty stomach. She hadn't been able to eat or drink a thing all shift—not even a frigging cup of coffee. But then, tonight she hadn't needed caffeine to keep her awake.

Conner caught her eye as he entered the room and gave her his usual grin—the same quirky yet charming grin that had won her heart, when he'd been transferred to the Twentieth Precinct a year ago.

They'd dated exclusively for six months before he'd suggested they move in together. Three months later, he'd proposed. She had been walking-on-air happy.

And so deluded.

Kate placed both hands over her stomach as it threatened to contract violently. This wasn't the time to get sick. Not the place, either.

Max left his desk and went to talk to Conner. Dan Bogart also joined them. The three guys had been buddies since their police academy days. Of the three, Conner was the only one in a serious relationship and sometimes she'd sensed that he missed the good old days of going to bars with his friends and chatting up women. But she'd never thought he would actually—

Kate bent her head over paperwork that she'd already completed. From the corner of her eye she observed the three friends. She saw Conner wink. Max faked a punch to Conner's shoulder and Dan laughed.

It hit her then.

They know.

The skin on her face tingled, the way it always did when her intuition kicked in. Pushing aside her reports and dropping her pen, she moved. The guys looked at her like nothing was wrong. Their innocent act didn't fool her. They'd actually had the nerve to laugh right in front of her.

How long had they known? Right from the beginning?

Maybe it was worse than simply knowing. Maybe they had worked as Conner's spies, letting him know when she was safely out of range so he could—

A wave of anger washed away her usual prudence. She'd planned to talk to Conner after his shift was over and they were at home.

But to hell with that. If everyone already knew, then privacy didn't matter, did it?

"So, boys, what's the big joke?"

"No joke, babe. We were just talking." Conner leaned in for a kiss, but she took a step away from him.

"I had a chat with Janet Beaker on my way to work this evening."

Right away Conner knew. She saw comprehension flash in his shifty eyes, then his expression grew guarded. "Let's talk about Janet later, okay? Come on, babe. I'll treat you to breakfast before you go home."

He moved closer, blocking Max and Dan from the conversation. She stepped aside.

"Max? Dan? You're part of this, right? I'm sure you want to be included now, as well."

The guys looked terrified, shaking their heads with a vehemence that only proved her suspicions.

Kate was vaguely aware that the room had grown dead quiet. But she was on the attack now. She couldn't stop.

"So who is she, Conner?" Kate tried to pin him with her gaze, but the coward would no longer look at her. "From Janet's description, I'm guessing Emily White in Records." She looked from Conner, to Max, then to Dan. She could tell by their sheepish expressions that she'd come up with the right woman.

"I saw the three of you, joking and congratulating yourselves. You seem to be pretty proud, but I'm not sure why anyone would think it's so great to be a liar and a cheat."

"Ouch," Max said. "Come on, Kate, give the guy a chance."

Kate's hands were fists, and the anger inside her was

hot, irrepressible. She had been so crazy about Conner. She'd really thought he cared as much about her as she did about him. Hell, they'd made love just before she went on duty. And only hours later, he'd invited someone else to their bed.

How could you? she wanted to cry. But years of police training and experience held her in good stead, allowing her to maintain a degree of emotional distance.

"Kate, you know I love you—"

She shook her head. "No. You don't get to say that anymore. Not after what you did."

"But—"

"I guess I'm just lucky I found out before the wedding." And before she'd had kids. God, what a mess this situation would be if children were involved. Kate drew in a shaky breath, then held her hand over a trash can. Unclenching her fist, she watched as the ring that had been a symbol of her happiness was swallowed up by the remains of somebody's midnight snack.

"KATE, STOP. I WANT TO TALK to you."

At the sound of her commanding officer's voice, Kate froze. Damn, she'd almost made it out of the building in one piece. Her legs were shaking. In fact, she thought every part of her body was about to give out on her. "Sir, this isn't a good time."

"No, I guess not. Still…get in here." He opened the door to a small meeting room and after a brief hesitation, she preceded him inside.

Lieutenant Rock was very tall with rough features

and a deep love of his job. Over the years, Kate had established a good rapport with the man, but right now she wasn't up to talking to *anyone*.

She wrapped her arms around her body, refusing a chair when he suggested they sit.

Rock rested his hands behind his back and sighed. "I heard what happened and—"

"Already?"

"Kate, everyone on the floor heard. As soon as people clued in to what was going down, the whole department could figure out that the shit was about to hit the fan."

"They figured that out pretty quickly, then. Maybe because most of them already knew." Kate wondered how many others had been privy to Conner's affair. These were supposed to be her colleagues and friends, too, not just his. And yet no one had said a word to her. She'd had to be clued in by a neighbor who had noticed Conner in the laundry room with another woman.

How sweet that Emily White had helped him wash the sheets and towels after… Oh, God. She blocked the awful images of the man she loved being with a woman who she *knew* didn't mean that much to him.

Why would he have risked everything they'd had— their love, their future—for a silly fling?

"He's a bloody fool, but the truth is, he was never good enough for you, Kate."

"I appreciate the sentiment, Lieutenant."

"It's sincere. I've got your back on this, so let's make a plan. Want me to transfer Lowery's butt out of here?"

"No." She'd been thinking about what she wanted to do. She'd intended to sleep on it before making a firm decision.

But nothing else had gone according to plan this morning, so what the hell. "I'm quitting."

"Get out, Cooper. You can't be serious. With your record? I'm sure I don't have to remind you that you're coming up for promotion."

"It wasn't just Conner who betrayed me. They all knew what was going on. Even my partner."

"You can't be sure of that."

She looked at him skeptically. As if.

"Kate, he's just a guy. You can't let one jerk change your life like this."

Rock didn't understand. She'd lost more than the man she loved today. She'd lost the biggest, most important dream of her life…the chance to start a family of her own. A warm, loving, happy family with lots of children and maybe a dog or a kitten thrown into the mix. Only twelve hours ago, she'd thought this was Conner's dream, as well.

But maybe he'd also been lying about that.

"If you really want a change, how about you put in for a transfer? I'd hate to lose you, but if it's what you want…"

She shook her head no. She'd always enjoyed her job, but after today, she couldn't imagine coming back here, or starting fresh with another group of strangers. "Remember Lindsay Fox and Nathan Fisher? They've been trying to convince me to come and work with them. Maybe I will."

"This isn't the time to be making life-altering decisions. Why don't you take a few days off? See how you feel when you've had a chance to cool down?"

Kate already knew how she'd feel. Betrayed. Hurt. Angry.

None of that was going to change.

When she made up her mind, she seldom changed it. And her mind was made up.

"I'm quitting. It's a done deal."

AS SOON AS SHE GOT HOME, Kate wrote her letter of resignation, then dropped it in the mail. She'd really felt a sense of pride working for the NYPD, but she had no sense of regret about leaving.

She had learned a lot from the organization, but she was ready to move on.

Next she packed all of Conner's belongings and arranged for a moving company to pick them up the next day. She called Conner at work to ask where he wanted her to send them.

"Kate, damn it, why are you moving so fast? We haven't even talked."

"Did you sleep with Emily White?"

"Stop it. We need to meet in person…"

"Why? So you can try to charm me? Forget it, Conner. Nothing will work. You haven't just lost my love and my trust. You've lost my respect. I don't want to see or speak to you again."

Her words were cutting and possibly cruel, but at least Conner got the message.

"Fine. Be that way, Kate. You can send my stuff to Max's apartment."

And that was it. The end of a one-year relationship.

Kate put down the phone, wondering if she was going to break down and cry. It hadn't happened yet. Oddly, once the first rush of anger had worn off, she'd felt quite calm.

The tears would come, she was certain, but while she was waiting she would clean the apartment. When she found a pair of Emily's pink panties between the mattress and the footboard, she was glad she'd gone to the effort.

"Disgusting." She put on a pair of rubber gloves, then carried them outside to the garbage chute. In the hallway she met Janet.

"You were right about Conner," she said.

"I'm sorry. Maybe I shouldn't have said anything?"

"I'm glad you did."

Only once her apartment was spotless, and the movers had arrived to remove Conner's belongings, was Kate able to sleep. She was out for over twelve hours and when she awoke, it was a new day.

She sat up in bed and checked in on her emotions. Was she going to cry now? But she felt not just calm, but peaceful. Maybe on a subconscious level she'd already known Conner wasn't the right man for her.

She was also hungry.

Kate spent the day indulging herself. She went out for breakfast, read the *New York Times* cover to cover, then strolled through Central Park. It was early March, cold and damp, but she thought she could feel springtime in the air—until a few flakes of snow landed on her nose.

She picked up some Thai takeout and rented a movie. Before watching it, however, she decided she'd better call her friend Lindsay Fox.

Lindsay had once worked with her at the Twentieth Precinct. Several years ago, she'd left to start a private investigation company on the Upper West Side, and routinely tried to convince Kate to join her.

Hopefully that offer was still open. She dialed the new number Lindsay had given her after she'd moved in with her partner—and now lover—Nathan Fisher.

Lindsay answered right away. "Kate, is that you?"

"You know that job you keep offering me…?"

Lindsay laughed. "Are you serious?"

"Yeah. I've had it with the NYPD."

"What put you over the edge? Midnight shifts? Having to be respectful to senior officers even when they're full of crap? Needing to fill out a form just to go to the frigging can?"

"All of the above. Oh, and plus I found out Conner was screwing a woman in Records."

"What?"

"It's true. Our engagement is over. I've returned the ring, kicked him out and I'm looking for a fresh start. And I mean a *totally* fresh start."

"Oh, Kate, I'm so sorry to hear that. What a flipping jerk, though."

"Yeah. I busted him right at the office, in front of all his buddies."

Lindsay whooped. "Serves him right."

"And then I told Rock I was quitting."

"Girl, I like your style. And you definitely called at the right time. Nathan and I are drowning in work. If we don't find someone soon, our sex life is going to be on permanent hold."

"That sounds desperate. So Nathan's a full-fledged partner now, is he?"

"I've even had new signs and business cards printed with Fox & Fisher. It's going well, Kate. Really well."

"I'm glad. You both deserve to be happy." Lindsay and Nathan took very different approaches to their jobs. Lindsay was all about gut-feel and action, whereas Nathan preferred methodical research and careful planning. Their skill sets were complementary, and Kate liked them both very much. More than that, she respected them and trusted them.

"Kate, I'm sorry for what you've been through. But I've always felt you'd be a perfect fit to work with Nathan and me."

Kate had the same feeling. "So when do I start?"

"I'd like to say tomorrow, but I have a partner now. I should probably arrange a meeting with you, me and Nathan. I'll call you later to set up a time."

JAY SAVAGE FINISHED HIS set of twelve reps, then replaced the weights on the rack. He was glad his buddy Nathan Fisher had talked him into going to the gym tonight.

He hadn't worked out once since his sister died and the physical release was just what he needed.

"Want to grab a beer after we've showered?" Nathan asked as they completed a slow lap around the track to cool off.

Jay checked the time. He had an hour before Eric's school night curfew of ten o'clock. "Okay, but it has to be quick."

They both had damp hair when they perched on bar stools fifteen minutes later. Always health conscious, Nathan asked for a Coors light, but Jay ordered a Guinness, figuring his workout justified the extra calories.

"So—how are you doing?" Nathan asked.

He'd attended Tracy's funeral a month ago and he'd called pretty much every week since then to check in. Jay appreciated his friend's concern, but he couldn't talk about what Tracy's death meant to him, the deep remorse he felt and the guilt.

"I'm doing okay, but I'm worried about Eric. Hell, even before his mother died I was concerned about him." At fourteen, Eric was at a critical age. Two years ago, he'd been a cheerful kid, eager to please. Now he was silent and moody, and Jay feared he was on the verge of making some very poor choices.

Just like Tracy had when she was his age.

"He must miss his mother," Nathan said.

"I'm sure he does, but he doesn't talk about her. I think he resents having to live with me." But there was no one else, so neither one of them had a choice in the matter.

"Maybe he needs time to adjust."

"Yeah. We both do." Eric had been furious with him when he'd imposed a curfew, but so far he was honoring it. Jay didn't think he was doing quite as well about school. He was pretty sure Eric had been cutting classes. He had an appointment set up this week with his home-room teacher to see if he was right.

"He's lucky he has you."

Jay nodded, but in truth he wasn't so sure about that. He'd practically raised his sister on his own, and look how she'd turned out. He didn't want to screw up with his nephew, too.

"Have you decided what you're going to do about work?"

Jay sighed. "My leave is over this week. I'm afraid I'm going to have to resign."

"Jeez, man, I'm sorry."

Nathan knew how much he loved flying. But when you worked as a commercial pilot, you had to be pre-pared to be away from home for three- or four-day stretches of time. With no backup at home for Eric, he just couldn't do that.

"Eric's too young to be alone overnight. And I can't afford live-in help." Jay tried to put a positive spin on the situation. "In a couple of years, when Eric's older, I'll go back."

"What are you going to do in the meantime?"

Jay shrugged. "Good question."

"We're looking for someone at the agency," Nathan said casually.

"Yeah?"

"Remember that summer we worked for Power Investigations?"

Jay laughed. "I haven't thought about that in years."

"We were staked out in that van, and it was so bloody cold."

"I was determined to make us coffee with that old propane stove—"

"And the curtains caught fire. Remember how that gray-haired guy came running from his garage with a garden hose?"

"Yeah, in his underwear. And his wife yelling at him from the front door…"

They were both laughing too much to continue with the story. Their cover had been so blown that night. Plus, the interior of the van had been badly damaged. For some reason Power hadn't fired them, though.

Jay wiped a tear from the corner of his eye. "Yeah, that was some job, all right."

"We raked in a pile of dough that summer."

"True." Enough money that they'd both been able to enroll in college that fall. Nathan to study criminology and Jay aviation flight training.

The two men drank their beers quietly for a moment. Finally Jay said, "You really have an opening?"

"You bet. Lindsay and I have been turning away clients lately because we just can't handle any more."

"You think Lindsay would agree to hire me even though I have no police training?"

"All that's really necessary for this job is the ability to think fast on your feet. You should see some of the characters we've interviewed for the position. If you're interested, come to the office and we'll talk. How about tomorrow at ten?"

Jay finished his beer. He couldn't believe how much better he felt now than when he'd left to meet Nathan two hours ago. The workout, the laughter, the friendship…he'd needed them all.

And now, on top of all that, Nathan was offering him a job. A job that might just be the perfect thing.

"I'm interested."

CHAPTER TWO

JAY SAVAGE WAS INFINITELY more comfortable traveling above the ground than below it. As the subway car swayed to the right, his body swayed left, knocking his legs into the knees of the seated lady beside him. She glared.

"Sorry." He'd given up his place for the old gal. Some gratitude.

He glanced at his nephew beside him. Eric moved with the rhythm of the train, as if they were part of the same entity—much like a cowboy on a horse. He waited for Eric to acknowledge his presence, but Eric's gaze was unmoving and unseeing.

Presumably his attention was all on the music playing on his iPod. The wires of his headphones led from his backpack and disappeared under the black wool of the hat he wore pulled over his embarrassing blond curls. At least Jay assumed Eric found those curls embarrassing, since he wore his hat almost all the time.

The train stopped at Cathedral Parkway, and as Eric swung forward, Jay tapped his shoulder. "Have a good day at school."

Eric just ignored him, disappearing amid a herd of

other middle-school-aged kids. Jay waited for the rush to end before slipping out and catching the next train headed south.

He didn't know why he bothered to ride the subway with Eric every morning. His nephew never talked to him. He supposed he just wanted to make sure he really was going to school. When Tracy was fourteen she'd skipped more days of school than she'd actually attended. He didn't want her son making the same mistake.

Jay exited the subway at the stop for the Museum of Natural History. The offices of Fox & Fisher were just a few blocks west. He was looking forward to finding out more about this job Nathan had promised him. He'd been dreading finding a new career, but this one sounded like it could be interesting, and he'd be glad to be working with Nathan, whom he both liked and respected.

And though the agency was small, with only two partners, just this September one of their cases had made the front page of the *Daily News*. So they were doing good work. Important work.

When Jay made his way up to ground level, he was greeted with a gray sky. Two-day-old snow was now sludge in the gutters. March wasn't the city's prettiest month, but he supposed April would be here before he knew it.

February had certainly passed quickly enough. Looking back now, the days were a blur of sadness and grief and endless, unhappy chores. He'd had to sublet Tracy's apartment, sell her furniture and settle her financial affairs. Then there'd been the business of moving Eric to his apartment and trying to make the kid feel at home.

Jay crossed the street and hurried along West Seventy-ninth Street until he came to the old brownstone where Fox & Fisher was located. A half flight of stairs led to the main door and a small vestibule with mailboxes and a door leading off to a hallway and more stairs.

Nathan went up another story and found yet another hallway. The door on the right had a new copper name-plate etched with The Fox & Fisher Detective Agency.

He took a deep breath, as if he was about to plunge into a cold lake, then opened the door.

A pretty brunette sat behind a modern, slate-gray desk. She smiled, waved him inside, then continued with the conversation she was having on the phone.

He glanced around. The all-business, ultramodern decor was softened by the presence of lots of green, healthy plants. An inviting array of magazines were spread out on a coffee table near a sofa and two arm-chairs. There was a bowl of jelly beans there, too.

Jay sat in one of the chairs—made of molded metal, yet surprisingly comfortable—and reached for the candies.

He looked up when the door opened again—this time admitting a tall woman about his age, dressed in a cream-colored trench coat. From this angle, all he could see was long, reddish-blond hair and a thin, elegant body.

With businesslike strides, she approached the recep-tionist and placed a hand on her desk.

"I'm here to see Lindsay Fox."

Her voice was deep and sexy and he gave the woman

a second glance. If this was an example of the kind of clients they had at Fox & Fisher, then he was all in.

The receptionist—Nadine Kimble, according to the nameplate he'd just noticed beside a small flowering plant—held up a hand for the woman to wait, then finally ended her call with a timid promise to phone back at the first chance. She set down the phone, then said, "I'll call Lindsay for you, but would you please wait a minute? The gentleman was here first."

The redhead turned to face him, then. "Sorry. I didn't see you." Her gaze swept over him with almost professional efficiency.

He was struck by how pretty she was. She reminded him, superficially, of Nicole Kidman, except that her skin wasn't pale porcelain like the actor's but flooded with freckles. The cute splotches of pigment only made her look more beautiful.

"Mr. Savage?"

He blinked as he realized the receptionist was trying to get his attention. "Yes."

"Nathan is waiting for you. I'm sorry I didn't greet you when you came in, but I was talking to my mother and if I'd interrupted her, well, let's just say it's never a good idea."

He immediately decided he loved this receptionist.

"Just take that door to the left, Mr. Savage. And good luck."

"HE LOOKS LIKE a football player," Kate said. She ignored the chair that Lindsay had invited her to sit in and went, instead, to check out the view from the window, which happened to be of a brick wall.

"Quarterback or lineman?"

"What?" Kate supposed the view didn't matter. She wouldn't be in the office much, anyway. She turned back to survey the decor, which she approved of. Modern, calming and most of all…practical. When it came to work, she didn't like to waste time and that was the message behind all this functional metal and glass furniture.

"Do you think Jay Savage looks like a quarterback or a lineman?"

Lindsay seemed amused. Kate was not. She hadn't expected there would be competition for this job. When she'd seen that man in the waiting room, she'd assumed he must be a client.

A very distinguished-looking client, with magnetic blue eyes and a commanding presence. "How should I know? He's big, all right. He'd never blend into a crowd on surveillance. A good investigator needs to blend in."

Lindsay didn't look convinced. "You're quite a bit taller than average, too, you know. And redheads always stand out in a crowd."

Kate was about to argue that she knew how to appear shorter, but realized how ridiculous that would sound. The truth was, she felt nervous.

Until ten minutes ago, she'd assumed the job was hers for the asking, that this "interview" was simply a formality. Just her luck that Nathan had offered the job to his buddy the same night she'd contacted Lindsay.

If only she'd phoned Lindsay sooner.

Jay Savage may not have her qualifications, but he wasn't the sort of man you could easily write off. He had an air of confidence and competence about him. He seemed like someone who was used to being in a situation of authority. A man who could do pretty much anything he put his mind to.

"You say he's a pilot? Is he even qualified for this job?"

"Well, he's a friend of Nathan's, and Nathan promised him an interview before I found out you were available, so we're kind of stuck having to consider him for the position." Lindsay passed her a file of case reports.

Kate leafed through them, the printed words a blur. "What's this?"

"I wanted to give you a flavor of the kind of work we do here at Fox & Fisher."

"I've read about two of your cases in the paper," Kate reminded her. In one instance, Lindsay had managed to locate a child rapist from the FBI's most wanted list. In the other, more recent case, she and Nathan had prevented a big-time property developer from murdering his wife. "Pretty exciting stuff."

"Believe me, those cases aren't typical of our usual clientele. You won't need to carry a gun—neither Nathan nor I do. The beauty of this job, though, is that unlike the police department, we don't have to take every case that comes our way. We can pick and choose."

"Tell me more."

"Why don't I just go through our list of open cases? Our work load right now is pretty typical." Lindsay clicked on a file on her computer, then twisted the screen so Kate could see, too. The jobs were mostly what Kate had expected. Locating missing persons, insurance fraud, background checks.

"You can set your own hours," Lindsay said, adding with a grin, "I can't remember the last time I had to work the midnight shift. Plus, you'll never see a doughnut in our office. Multigrain bagels with light cream cheese is Nathan's idea of a treat." She wrinkled her nose.

Kate laughed. "Where do I sign?"

"Start with this." Lindsay handed her a sheet of paper on a clipboard with a pen. "It's a standard job application. Fill it out, then we'll meet with Nathan and Jay in the boardroom."

"Nathan *and* Jay?"

"We decided we'd have a roundtable discussion. It was my idea. I figured you'd really shine if Nathan had a chance to compare you directly to Jay."

Kate wasn't so sure, but she couldn't admit to being fazed. "Fine. If that's what you want."

"We won't be making our final decision until later." Lindsay raked her fingers through her straight blond hair. "And don't worry. Nathan's a reasonable man…as you well know. In the end, he'll be forced to concede that you are far more qualified than his friend."

That made sense, Kate decided. She could see how Nathan was obligated to at least give Jay Savage a hearing. She sat down and began filling in the empty spaces, while Lindsay resumed work at her keyboard.

When she had the form completed, Kate passed it back to Lindsay.

Lindsay scanned it quickly. "Great. I'll call Nathan and let him know we're ready."

While Lindsay was on the phone, Kate popped a throat lozenge. Over the past couple of days she'd developed a tickle in her throat and she hoped she wasn't coming down with a cold. But given all she'd been through lately, she wouldn't be surprised if her immune system had quit on her.

"We're ready. You, too? Good." Lindsay disconnected the call, then stood. "Let's go get 'em, Kate."

"You bet." Kate held her head high as she followed Lindsay from her office to a room down the hall. They settled into chairs and Kate took quick stock of her surroundings. Like the rest of the office, the conference room was modern, minimalistic and monotone. On the wall were some odd-looking black-and-white photographs. After a few seconds, Kate realized they were close-ups of paper clips.

A moment later Nathan and Jay entered the room. Kate had hoped to discover that Jay's physical presence wasn't as impressive as she'd thought, but to her dismay, she felt the same jolt at seeing him the second time.

She tried to focus on Nathan, who had a warm, boy-next-door appeal that was much easier to handle. Though he looked to be as fit and agile as ever, his true strength lay in his brilliant mind. His new glasses only added to his charm.

Nadine appeared briefly to offer a choice of beverages. Kate opted for water, and once everyone had been served Nadine returned to the front desk, closing the door to give them privacy.

"So," Lindsay began. "Thank you, Kate, and Jay, for coming to talk with us today. I wish we could offer both of you a job, but unfortunately that isn't economically feasible right now."

"We'll start by laying out our expectations for the position," Nathan continued. "And then you guys can hit us with your questions."

A knock sounded at the door, then Nadine reentered the room, looking flustered. "I'm sorry to interrupt, but a woman named Hannah Young just came in. She says she made an appointment for ten-thirty with Lindsay. She's very adamant about not being able to wait."

It was twenty minutes to eleven now. Kate looked at Lindsay, who was shaking her head.

"I can't believe I forgot…" She put a hand to her chin, and her brow furrowed as she thought. A smile slowly appeared on her face. "Actually, this could be a good thing."

"What are you thinking?" Nathan asked. "I know that look and it makes me nervous."

"I've had the most brilliant idea. Nadine, tell Hannah I'll be right out to talk to her."

"What?" Nathan asked. "You're just going to keep us all waiting in here?"

"Not for long. On the phone Hannah told me that her budget is very tight. I may have come up with a solution to everyone's problems."

THE CONFERENCE ROOM FELL uncomfortably silent, as if Lindsay had sucked out all the energy when she left the room. Kate knew Lindsay well enough to be apprehensive about this "brilliant" idea of hers. She could tell Nathan and Jay felt the same way as they exchanged nervous glances.

"She hasn't changed, has she?" Kate asked.

"God help us all, no," Nathan agreed. He reached across the table and snagged the form Kate had recently filled out. Her job application seemed to absorb his attention, leaving Kate and Jay with little to look at but each other since there were no windows in the room and the only art on the walls were those pictures of paper clips.

Jay smiled. He had a really warm smile. And his eyes were the darkest blue she had ever seen. He wouldn't need to ask witnesses a single question, Kate thought. They would just talk.

She blinked, thinking of another man's smile, and all that it had been hiding. "So you're a pilot?"

"I am."

He was her competition. She might as well get to know him. "What do you fly?"

"Most recently Boeing 777s. But I've retired."

"So you want to shift from flying planes to private investigating?"

He nodded, as if it were the most usual career path anyone could imagine. "And I hear you used to work for the NYPD?"

"That's right." He had to realize how unmatched their qualifications were, but he didn't look worried in the least.

She had to admit, the guy had balls.

Lindsay flew back into the room then, with a young woman in tow.

"I'd like you to meet Hannah Young." Lindsay made her way around the room with introductions, then pulled out a chair for Hannah.

Kate took careful stock of the new client, who looked to be in her mid-twenties. Hannah was an attractive woman, dressed in a cheaply tailored skirt and blazer. She was a little hesitant about making eye contact, but her smile was pleasant. Her jewelry was silver—modest studs in her ears and a collection of rings on various fingers. The one on her wedding finger had a tiny diamond.

"Hannah and her husband are hoping to start a family," Lindsay began. She kept talking, but suddenly Kate couldn't focus.

Hannah was at least five years younger than she was, and here she was, married and about to have babies. Kate couldn't help but feel a deep, illogical jealousy.

If her relationship with Conner had worked out, if he had been the man she'd thought he was, she would have been in Hannah's position soon. Trying to get pregnant. Planning her maternity leave.

Now her dream of children seemed totally out of reach. She'd always thought she would have her first baby at thirty and she was already thirty-two.

Worst of all, the very idea of dating someone new was enough to make her ill.

"So what do you think?" Hannah asked. "Can your firm help us?"

To her dismay, Kate realized she'd lost focus and had no clue what the client wanted from Fox & Fisher. Fortunately Lindsay stepped in with an answer that summarized the client's needs.

"You want us to find your biological father so you can make sure there are no genetic problems in your family tree before you try to have a baby. No problem. We've handled this sort of case many times, haven't we, Nathan?"

"Absolutely," he said. "I assume you've never tried to find your real parents?"

"No. As far as I'm concerned, I already have real parents. My mom and dad are wonderful and if it wasn't for Jeremy and his worries, I probably would never have been interested in tracing my biological mother and father."

"Where is your husband right now?" Kate asked. If he was so concerned about his future baby's DNA, then why wasn't he at this meeting?

"He wanted to come," Hannah said, as if reading her mind, "except his boss is a real jerk about giving time off."

"What do you have to go on?" Kate asked. "Are your biological parents listed on your birth certificate? Have your adoptive parents given you the name of the adoption agency they used?"

Hannah seemed overwhelmed by the questions. She turned to Lindsay, who answered for her.

"Hannah's already located her birth mother. They've

met and everything checked out fine with that side of the family. The problem is locating the father."

"My birth mom got pregnant in her first term at college. Her parents had been really strict and as soon as she was out of the house, she went kind of wild." Hannah opened the big leather bag she'd been carrying and pulled out a yearbook from New England College. There were three yellow markers in the book and Hannah flipped pages to the first one.

"James Morgan was a guy Mom met during frosh week. He was studying business. She thinks."

She flipped to the next yellow tab. "Gary Gifford was on the football team, and finally…" She flipped more pages, to the last picture, a slight boy with protruding ears. "Oliver Crane was in her English 101 class. My real dad could be any one of these guys."

Three possibilities. Okay. "I'm assuming your mother didn't keep in touch with any of them?"

"No. She didn't see the point because she wasn't keeping the baby. Plus she was worried one of them would try to talk her out of her decision. Which wasn't very likely if you ask me. I mean, imagine you're a young guy in his first year of college. If you made a girl pregnant after a one-night stand, wouldn't you appreciate it if she handled the problem on her own?"

It wasn't fair, Kate thought, but Hannah was probably right.

"So—" Lindsay patted the yearbook "—we know where these guys were twenty-four years ago, but after that—nada. We're starting from scratch. First we need to locate these three men, then convince them to let us test their DNA for a match to Hannah's."

"We could get lucky and get a match on the first try," Nathan said. "Or, we could end up spending weeks and weeks on this."

"Which would add up to a bill that Hannah and Jeremy just can't afford," Lindsay said.

"We need to save our money for the baby." Hannah tugged on her earlobe anxiously. "But there won't be a baby until we're sure there aren't any genetic problems in my family tree."

"Here's the deal." Lindsay flattened her hands on the table and leaned forward. "I told Hannah we'd take the case pro bono, if she'd let us assign two novice investigators to the file."

Kate's interest shifted up a notch. "I'm assuming you mean Jay and me?"

Lindsay nodded.

Kate strongly objected to being called a "novice investigator," but for the moment she opted to keep quiet. Though she'd initially expected to be handed this job on a silver platter, now that she'd met the competition, the prospect of proving her skills on a specific case was intriguing.

"Pro bono, huh? That's a very generous offer." Nathan spoke quietly to his partner. "Are you sure you've thought this through?"

"You haven't heard the whole plan yet," Lindsay continued. "Before Hannah arrived, we were at an impasse. You wanted to hire Jay and I wanted to hire

Kate. My idea is to have both of them work independently on this. The first one to locate Hannah's biological father will, by definition, be the best investigator. That's the person who will get the job."

CHAPTER THREE

IT WAS AN OUTRAGEOUS proposition. But also…intriguing. There were few things Jay enjoyed more than healthy competition. Basketball and squash were his usual sports, but this sounded interesting. True, he didn't have Kate's training, but he was nothing if not resourceful.

If he found Hannah's father and got the job, there'd be classes to take, a license to acquire. Nathan had assured him that none of this would be too onerous. Before he knew it, he'd be launched in his second career.

Jay checked out Kate from across the table. She gave him a small smile, her eyes sharp and confident. Then she raised her eyebrows and cocked her head slightly.

The challenge was obvious—she didn't think he had a chance. And every nerve in his body ached to prove her wrong.

"This plan sounds crazy to me," Nathan said. "But if Hannah, Kate and Jay all agree, then I have no objection. Hannah, are you sure you want to turn the search for your father into a competition?"

"If it means I don't have to pay anything, then

yeah. You bet I do. I really want a baby and as long as I can tell Jeremy who my real dad is, I don't care who finds him."

"Okay," Nathan said. "The client agrees. How about you, Kate?"

She was still looking at Jay, with gray-green eyes that seemed to say, *Back out now and preserve your dignity.*

She raised her chin an inch higher. "I'm game."

Now everyone turned to him. He thought about what he had to lose. Not much, except his pride. Then he thought of what he could gain.

Nathan had been his friend since high school. Jay knew the guy had integrity and smarts. Lindsay seemed his polar opposite in many respects, but he could tell she had the same sense of honor, the same drive to make the world a better place.

If he couldn't fly planes anymore for a living, surely this was as good a place to land as any. Plus it would be fun to wipe that cocky expression from Kate Cooper's face.

He glanced around the room one more time, prolonging the moment of tension.

"I'm in."

Hannah clapped her hands together. "Thank you so much. I never dreamed that it would be this easy."

"We haven't found your father yet," Lindsay cautioned. She glanced at Kate, then smiled. "Though I'm sure it won't take very long."

She had a lot of confidence in her friend. Jay supposed it was to be expected. Meanwhile Nathan gave him a nod of encouragement which he appreciated.

"We'll be in touch with interim reports on Kate's and Jay's progress," Lindsay promised as she ushered Hannah to the door. She called Nadine and asked her to walk their new client through the usual paperwork.

"Plus, we'll need three DNA samples from her, Nadine. You know where we keep the kits…?"

Nadine must have answered in the affirmative, because Lindsay said, "Good. I'll leave you to it, then." She returned to the conference room, closing the door again.

"Well." She beamed at Nathan, her expression bordering on smug. "Was that a brilliant idea or what?"

Nathan shook his head. "I don't know whether to laugh or cry, frankly." But from the warmth in his voice, it was clear how he felt about Lindsay. He adored her. Jay could understand why. Lindsay was a dynamo. All passion and energy.

Her friend Kate, on the other hand, kept her emotions carefully contained. She seemed analytical and calculating and somewhat aloof. She was going to make a formidable opponent.

Also, a very beautiful one.

"The investigation will officially start tomorrow morning." Lindsay turned from Kate to Jay. "I'll have Nadine prepare a report for each of you containing all the information we have to date. Where you decide to start is completely up to you. Fair enough?"

"Absolutely," Jay said.

"Where will we work when we're not in the field?" Kate asked.

"We only have one empty office," Nathan said. "I

guess you'll have to share. We can bring in an extra desk and chair, but there's just one computer."

"No problem. I have a laptop." Jay stood and offered Kate his hand. "Good luck."

She hesitated, then stood as well and accepted his hand. "May the best investigator win."

No doubt she thought she would be the one. But she was in for a few surprises where he was concerned.

WITH THE MEETING CONCLUDED, Lindsay suggested to Kate that they go for a drink.

"That sounds good." Kate wasn't in a hurry to return to her empty apartment. She was going to have to get a cat, she decided, since she was no longer interested in men.

Lindsay led the way to a tired tavern just down the block. The Stool Pigeon was a knockoff on the traditional English pub concept, with a vague nod to Tudor architecture and an array of flea market atrocities displayed on shelves just out of dusting range.

A boisterous group in their twenties was sitting at the tables near the windows, and a dark brooding man presided over the three older male customers at the large oak bar. Brown vinyl booths at the back were all empty and that was where Lindsay led her.

"Nice place," Kate said, grimacing as she slid into the booth and her hand came in contact with something sticky.

"Cozy, isn't it? I come here all the time. This is Wendy."

Since she had her back to the kitchen, Kate hadn't noticed the female server approaching. The woman, in her mid-forties, seemed to have weathered about as well as the place where she worked.

"Wendy and Mark own this place," Lindsay explained.

"Lucky us," Wendy said drily. "I assume you want your usual?" When Lindsay nodded, she turned to Kate. "And you?"

"I'll have an orange juice with lots of ice." Hopefully the vitamin C would help ward off the cold she felt coming on.

"And fries," Lindsay added. "We'll share."

When the server returned a short time later, Kate was surprised to see that she'd brought Lindsay a paralyzer.

"You still drink those? How does your stomach tolerate them?" Once, when she and Lindsay had gone for a drink after a rough shift, she'd ordered one. A single swallow had been enough for her. She'd been shocked to find out what was in the drink. A motley mixture of liqueurs, cream and cola.

"My system runs on paralyzers," Lindsay assured her.

"So how are things with Nathan? They seem good."

"Better than good. I've never been happier."

"You look happy." Kate was sincerely glad for her friend.

"Thanks. I wish I could say the same to you. Tell me about Conner. What was his problem? Didn't he know how lucky he was to have you?"

"Thanks, Lindsay." Kate felt tears well up at her friend's kindness. "In some ways I've decided that it's a good thing that we broke up—though I would have wished for a more civilized finale."

"Sometimes a good drama is the only way to go. I'm glad you gave him a piece of your mind."

"I guess. But I've come to realize over the last few days I wasn't as much in love with Conner as I thought I was."

"Why do you say that?"

"I hate to admit this, but I think I just latched on to him because I was at the point where I wanted to get married."

"Why so keen to get married?"

"Babies. Ever since I turned thirty that's all I think about. Everywhere I go, I see them. Did you notice that woman with the stroller on our way here?"

"Yeah, but this is the Upper West Side. There are kids everywhere. I never knew you were so keen to have children."

"I've always wanted a big family as well as a challenging career," Kate confessed. "Not just one or two children. More like three or four."

"Wow…I guess you'll have to start dating, then."

Kate made a face. "Forget it. I've had enough of men for a while."

"So what are you thinking? You want to be a single mother?"

"Maybe. I've been considering it. What do you think? Am I crazy?" She picked up a fry and stared at it without any appetite.

"No, not crazy. But it's a serious step. Don't do anything rash." Lindsay ate another fry. "Anyway, I'm so glad you're here. I promise you'll be happy at our agency. The work is varied and interesting and you'll have so much more freedom than you did working for the NYPD."

"That's assuming I find Hannah's father first and get the job," Kate reminded her.

"Jay doesn't stand a chance of solving this case faster than you."

Kate had already told herself the same thing. But Jay Savage struck her as the sort of guy who wasn't used to losing. She had to make sure that, this time, he did.

THE NEXT MORNING Kate arrived at the agency bright and early. She forced herself to get out of bed, even though she'd had a restless night, thanks to that tickle at the back of her throat. No matter how many vitamins she popped or how much orange juice she drank, it would not go away.

She bumped into Nadine, who was unlocking the main door. The young receptionist gave her a welcoming smile. "Lindsay and Nathan don't usually come in until nine. You must be an early bird."

"When I need to be." Kate didn't care when Lindsay and Nathan arrived for work, but she sure hoped that Jay wouldn't be in for a while.

Nadine gave her a closer look. "Do you have a cold? There's a mean one going around. I had it last week and it was terrible."

"Just a tickle in my throat." She had no time to get sick, and so she wouldn't. Mind over matter. "Did Lindsay leave anything for me?"

"Yes. She asked me to prepare two files—one for you and one for Jay." Nadine unlocked the bottom drawer of her desk and pulled out a folder which she handed to

Kate. "I'm guessing you'd like to get straight to work. The office you're sharing with Jay is opposite the conference room. Call me if you need anything. And if you're a coffee drinker, I'll have a fresh pot ready in ten minutes."

"Thanks, Nadine." This receptionist of Lindsay's was so pleasant and helpful, especially when compared with some of the dispatchers Kate had worked with over the years.

With her leather bag slung on one shoulder, Kate's hands were free to open the folder as she walked. Inside she found a summary of the information Hannah had given them yesterday and copies of forms she must have filled out with Nadine.

Kate paused to open the door to her new office, then assessed the layout. A second desk had been squeezed next to a file cabinet. The original desk, in front of a window that looked out at—surprise!—a brick wall, was larger and also had the computer on it. She sat there.

She'd done a lot of thinking last night and already knew where she wanted to start: with Hannah's birth mother. Thankfully her name, phone number and address were included in the file. Rebecca Trotter lived in Brooklyn with her husband and two school-aged children.

It would be best to arrange a face-to-face meeting. There was a chance Hannah's mother would tell her things she wouldn't have felt comfortable sharing with her daughter. At any rate, Kate wanted to verify the list of father candidates before she went to the work of tracking them down.

Hoping to catch the woman before she left for work,

or to take the kids to school, depending on her routine, Kate dialed the home number provided in the file. A woman answered, sounding harried.

"Yes? Who is this?"

"Kate Cooper from The Fox & Fisher Detective Agency. Your birth daughter—"

"Fox & Fisher? Again? Look, I want to help, but I'm busy. I have two kids to get ready for school, breakfast to cook, lunches to make. I don't have time for this. I already told that nice man last night, afternoons are more convenient for me."

Oh my God. That nice man had to be Jay. And he'd already talked to Hannah's mother last night. Kate couldn't believe she had been scooped so quickly.

"I apologize. I didn't realize Jay had already set up a time for us to talk."

"He didn't mention anything about you coming along. Kate, was it?"

"Yes. Kate Cooper. It is actually important that we both speak with you, so to waste the least amount of your time, we should probably combine the interviews."

"Doesn't matter to me. Jay's coming here this afternoon at one. Does that work for you?"

"It sure does, Mrs. Trotter. Thank you very much."

AFTER A MORNING spent surfing for information on the alumni of New England College, Jay called for a cab to take him to Brooklyn. This morning he'd decided not to accompany Eric on the subway. Not that Eric seemed to care, one way or the other.

Jay was worried about all the emotions Eric must be bottling inside. One of the doctors who had been on duty the night Tracy died had suggested counseling for the boy, but Eric had walked out of the session Jay had arranged with a grief therapist. Jay didn't have any other ideas on how to handle the situation.

The poor kid had walked in on his unconscious mother. He'd called 9-1-1 and had waited alone in the hospital until he'd been told that his mother was dead.

It was more than most adults could bear, and Eric was just a kid.

Jay had been flying the night Tracy died, on the last leg of a transoceanic trip to Europe. He hadn't received the frightened message his nephew had left on his cell phone until the next day.

He wondered if Eric blamed him for not making it to the hospital in time. If so, he wouldn't be surprised. He certainly blamed himself. Too late he realized he'd pursued his dream of flying at the expense of his family's best interests. He should have kept closer tabs on his sister and her son. No doubt about that.

Still, the mistakes he'd made in the past didn't change the reality of his problems with Eric. This past month he'd let a lot of things slide. Not just rudeness, but a general sloppiness around the apartment. He had to start laying down some ground rules with the boy, which he knew wouldn't go over well.

Tracy had never been one for rules, or discipline of any type.

Jay sighed at the prospect of what lay ahead. Sometimes it was hard for him to believe Eric was the same child that he had watched grow up from infancy. He'd done a lot of babysitting for Tracy over the years, and Eric had always loved spending time with him.

They'd done stuff like feed the ducks at Central Park and ride the ferry on the Hudson. He'd taught Eric to skate and to ride a bike. And yet, at some point Eric had stopped seeing him as his favorite person in the world.

He'd heard his colleagues at work, the ones with families, complain about what happened when kids became teenagers. He supposed it was the same with Eric. After all, Tracy had changed a lot when she'd hit adolescence, too.

For now he'd just keep doing his best to make his nephew comfortable in his new home. He'd already converted the office in his apartment into a second bedroom, he'd bought a Wii and set up a computer for the boy to use in the family room.

Still, nothing he'd done seemed to have softened Eric's attitude toward him. He had a meeting scheduled with his homeroom teacher this afternoon. Maybe she would have some useful advice.

"What's the address again?" the driver asked him. They were crossing the bridge into Brooklyn, the Statue of Liberty dimly visible to the south.

Jay answered, then told himself to stop thinking about his nephew and start focusing on the job. He needed to be sharp if he wanted to best Kate Cooper, and so far he liked to think he was off to a fast start.

Ten minutes later the driver pulled up in front of the

Trotters' address. The home Rebecca shared with her husband and two kids was one in a long line of attached houses, with a garage out front and a tiny lawn.

Jay paid the driver, arranged a pick-up time, then made his way to the front door. It was exactly one o'clock when he rang the bell.

The woman who came to the door had to be Rebecca Trotter, since she looked like an older, fifteen-pound-heavier version of Hannah. Amazing the power of genetics. He smiled and said hello. "Jay Savage. We spoke on the phone last night."

"You're finally here. Come on in. We're in the kitchen."

Finally? We? He checked his watch and wondered if it was running slow. They passed through a small living room, with toys and books strewn on the carpet, to a kitchen crammed with more toys and a large pine table.

Sitting in one of the chairs facing him was Kate Cooper, looking very pleased with herself.

"Hi, Jay. Glad you could make it."

CHAPTER FOUR

THE EXPRESSION ON JAY'S face was priceless. Kate hoped she was going to see a lot of that look in the weeks to come, though she had to admit she was impressed at how fast he'd been coming out of the gate.

Rebecca invited Jay to sit down and offered him a cup of coffee. He noticed the pitcher of filtered water and glasses on the table and declined.

"Water's fine by me."

"Let's get started then," Rebecca said. "My shift at the hospital starts at three. I'm a nurse," she explained in an aside to Jay, having already told Kate earlier.

"We were just talking about Rebecca's reaction when her daughter asked to meet her," Kate said, easing Rebecca back on topic. "It must have been the most shocking phone call of your life."

"It was a surprise. A wonderful surprise. I'd always hoped that one day my daughter would contact me. And it was amazing to finally meet her. Pretty, isn't she? Sweet, too." Rebecca smiled, a little proud, a little regretful. "Frankly, I'd hoped she would get in touch sooner. But I'm glad she was so happy with her adoptive parents that she didn't feel the need to."

"Were you worried about your husband's reaction to meeting her?" Kate asked.

"Not at all. John knows the whole story. I met him in October, about a month after I got pregnant, though I didn't realize I was carrying a baby at the time. When I finally clued in to the fact that I hadn't had a period in a while, I was up-front with him. I was terrified. Didn't have a clue what to do. I knew my parents would be furious if I told them."

"So you didn't?" Kate asked.

"No. John gallantly offered to marry me on the spot—but I felt we were too young. Still he helped me get through the rest of the school year, and his family put me up for the holidays. Then, after the baby was born, they organized the adoption. My parents never had a clue."

"John sounds like an amazing guy," Jay said.

"Oh, he is, but no one's perfect, right? He made his share of mistakes as a teenager. My wild and crazy phase lasted all of one month. Getting pregnant at eighteen tends to make you grow up fast."

"I imagine it does. And now your daughter is married and planning to have children of her own," Jay said. "Must be hard to believe."

"You're not kidding. I understand her husband wanting to know about Hannah's father. And I'm willing to help any way I can. But after all these years, I'm not sure it will be possible."

"You never talked to any of those guys once you realized you were pregnant?" Kate asked.

"I wasn't planning to keep the baby, so I didn't see the point. It wasn't like I had a relationship with any of them." Her face pinkened. "I must admit I'm a little embarrassed, now, that I slept with three different guys in one month— more like one week, to be honest. But I was caught up with the excitement of being on my own for the first time in my life. Frosh week was so exciting. There were so many parties, with drinking and…well, you know."

Kate nodded sympathetically. She wasn't inclined to judge the other woman poorly for her behavior. In fact, she admired Rebecca for having the gumption to return to school and earn her degree after the baby. Clearly she was a hardworking, responsible wife and mother now. And she was willing to do whatever she could to help Hannah.

Kate pulled out the photocopied pages from the college yearbook and placed them in front of Rebecca. "Hannah told us that these are the three men who might be her father. I'd like to confirm that with you, and also ask if you can remember anything else about them?"

"I'm sorry. I told Hannah everything I know."

"The smallest detail might be helpful," Jay said. "Since you were all new to college and each other, the guys might have mentioned where they were from?"

Kate looked up sharply. He'd taken her general question and redirected it to something specific. For a guy with no training, he had smart instincts.

"Oh. Funny you should say that." Rebecca took a closer look at the photograph of James Morgan. "I remember Jimmy talking about his family's lake resort.

I'm pretty sure he said it was somewhere in Upper New York State. Once he'd finished his business degree he was planning to go back and run it."

"That's exactly the sort of detail we're looking for," Jay encouraged. "Can you possibly recall the name of the lake?"

She wrinkled her forehead. "I'm sorry. It was so long ago."

"That's okay. This is a great help." Kate jotted down the details in the fresh notepad she'd started for this case. Too bad Jay had learned the exact same information that she had. But she would find that lake before he did. She was determined that she would.

She and Jay quizzed Rebecca about the other two men, hoping to unlock more forgotten tidbits of information, but Hannah's birth mother couldn't come up with anything else helpful.

"I already told Hannah that Gary was on the football team. He was a big guy, like you," she said, glancing at Jay. "I can't think of anything else unique about him. As for Oliver, he was very quiet. We didn't talk much at all." She laughed a little self-consciously. "I'm sorry I can't be more help. These were obviously one-night hookups."

Kate passed her a card with her name and number. "That's fine. We appreciate your time. Please call if you remember anything else. No matter how trivial."

Jay looked flummoxed, and she hid a smile. He could hardly pass his own number on to Rebecca now and ask her to call him, as well. Rebecca would assume Kate

C.J. CARMICHAEL

53

would pass along any information to Jay. Which, of course, she would definitely *not* do.

As they made their way to the front door, Rebecca chattering about her kids and apologizing for the mess, Jay brushed by Kate and whispered, "Very clever."

His breath was warm, and she shivered as his arm touched hers. She was a tall woman, but he was much taller, and his broad, football-player shoulders were solid muscle.

Out on the street, a cab was waiting.

"Want to share?" Jay offered. "I assume you're heading back to the office?"

"I took the subway here and was planning to go back the same way." She hesitated, for some reason reluctant to be in close quarters, alone—the driver didn't count—with this guy. But wasn't that foolish? The more she knew about Jay, the more likely she could find his weakness.

"But since you're already paying the fare…" She climbed into the back and he joined her.

As he gave the address to the driver, then settled back into his seat, it struck her how surreal their situation was. In one day this man had gone from being a total stranger to her rival in one of the strangest competitions she had ever been a part of.

Who was Jay Savage? Suddenly she was curious. What were his interests? What was his background? Was there a woman in his life?

He struck her as the sort of man who would have lots of women hanging around. Or was that just an unfair stereotype of an attractive, unmarried pilot? Or her own sour grapes after Conner's betrayal?

He caught her eye. "It was quite a surprise to find you at Rebecca Trotter's."

She couldn't help smiling. That had been a sweet moment, all right. "I plan to keep surprising you. Maybe you should just quit now."

His laugh was low and sensual. "I don't think so. Technically I got to Rebecca Trotter first."

"About that. Rebecca said you called her last night. But according to the rules, our investigation wasn't supposed to start until this morning."

"I didn't think arranging an interview counted as 'investigating.' Last night I did a little searching through some phone directories. When I saw the Trotters' number, I figured it couldn't hurt to call."

She didn't recall even hearing Hannah's birth mother's name. Perhaps it had been mentioned when she'd been zoning out. That would teach her to daydream during important meetings.

"I suppose that's fair enough."

He frowned. "I hope you mean that. I intend this to be an honest competition."

He sounded sincere and Kate appreciated that.

"Believe me," he continued, "I didn't even think that I was breaking the rules of our competition when I called Rebecca last night. I was trying to be organized."

"If I'd have thought of it, I probably would have called her, too," Kate conceded. "Still, it gave you the advantage."

"You think? You're the one who left Rebecca your

number, not me. If she remembers something else, I'm not likely to hear about it, am I?"

"No."

He smiled. "At least you're honest."

"It wouldn't be much of a competition if we shared information with one another. I feel it's only fair to tell you—I really want this job. I kind of burned my bridges with the NYPD."

With hindsight, the letter of resignation she'd written could have been drafted with a bit more tact. Not that she planned to ever go back. But she'd shut that door a bit more forcefully than was really necessary.

"Why? Was it the stress?"

"Partly it was the hours. Partly my impatience with the bureaucracy."

"But there's more to the story," he guessed.

He was easy to talk to. Too easy. She wondered if he was just passing the time, or if he was really interested. Know the enemy… Was that his strategy, too?

Still, she had no reason to be secretive. "I just ended a long-term relationship. And I'm ready for a change in my life. I want to try new things. Go new places."

"Meet new people?" he suggested. "Maybe have a rebound affair?"

She caught a subtle lift to his voice, and narrowed her eyes at him. Was it possible Jay was flirting with her? She glanced at him again. The man was easy to talk to, but not easy to read.

"I'm not interested in any sort of affair. Rebound or otherwise."

"Maybe it's too soon. Since your breakup, I mean."

Yes, it was soon, but Kate couldn't imagine changing her mind for a long time. "What about you? Are you in a relationship?"

He shrugged. "There's no one serious. I tend to avoid that sort of thing."

"So the stereotype of the single, male pilot fits after all. A girl in every city…is that how it works?"

"Hardly *every* city. I don't have that much energy."

She refused to smile. "It's going to be difficult to keep the women in line now that you're stuck in one place. What's with that, anyway? Why the switch from pilot to P.I.?"

"Like you, I have plenty of reasons. But the main one is my nephew, Eric. I need to be home in the morning to get him off to school. And I want to be home every evening to cook dinner and make sure he does his schoolwork. It may sound mundane to you, but I'm his only family now."

It didn't sound mundane at all. It sounded like what she had wanted—and still did. "You can't be a caregiver for your nephew and a pilot at the same time?"

"As a single parent it would be difficult. I was a long-haul, international pilot. I could have requested shorter routes, but even those require you to be away from home for three- or four-day stretches."

"Will you miss flying?"

His eyes darkened. "No question."

Yet, he'd given it up for his nephew. She admired that. "Did you ever run into trouble during a flight? Something serious, that you didn't think you'd survive?"

He blinked, then gazed out at the passing city. "The vast majority of flights are pretty routine. And thank God for that. No one in their right mind would get into a commercial airliner otherwise."

She looked at him closely. "You just sidestepped my question."

"You think?" He smiled disarmingly. "What about you? Did you ever run into big trouble in your job at the Twentieth Precinct? Something you didn't think you'd survive?"

"A couple of times, yes. But it's the cases that break your heart that are more difficult to handle."

Jay's expression grew serious. "Yeah. It's hard to see someone suffer. Even when they've done it to themselves."

"What always gets me is how fast it happens. One minute everything is good. The next—catastrophe."

"Maybe one night, when this is all over, we'll get together and exchange war stories," he said.

"Maybe."

She felt relieved that the taxi was pulling up in front of the office. Jay was more complicated than she'd initially thought, more intelligent and more sensitive, too. And he had skills she hadn't expected.

Consider how easily he'd extracted that information about the lake resort from Rebecca.

And how quickly he'd extracted information about her, as well.

CHAPTER FIVE

IT WAS GOING TO BE interesting sharing an office with Kate, Jay thought. She'd already claimed the big desk by the window, which was fair enough, since she needed the computer. Still, sitting at the smaller desk by the door meant that she could see his computer screen every time she got up to get a coffee.

"Oh, stop being so paranoid." Kate squeezed past him with a steaming mug in hand. "I'm not trying to sneak a look at your computer every time I walk by."

"Maybe you should be. Might save you some valuable time."

"Very funny, *Captain*. Hope you're prepared for some turbulence ahead." She grinned. "How are you liking your new desk? Not much room for your legs, huh?"

She wasn't kidding. He'd only been here an hour and he could already feel his muscles cramping. "Well, at least I have a good view of yours."

Her eyes widened, and she quickly uncrossed her legs and pulled down on her skirt. "You shouldn't be looking."

"Why not? Beats the view out the window."

"What? You don't like brick walls?"

"I live in New York. I love brick walls."

She cracked a smile at that, then took a sip from her mug and leaned closer to her computer screen. "Keep quiet now. I've got to concentrate."

He should be doing the same. Only she was fun to talk to. She had an interesting mind, and a sly sense of humor that he rather enjoyed.

Anyway, he'd already found where prospective dad number one, James Morgan, lived. All he'd had to do was type "vacation resort," "Upper New York State" and "James Morgan" into his favorite search engine.

Now he needed to rent a car. Taking his mug with him, and closing the door firmly on the sound of Kate's clattering on the keyboard, he headed for the reception area to talk to Nadine.

As he'd guessed on the first day, Nadine was a real sweetheart. Quick to smile and anxious to please.

"Hi, Jay. The coffee is fresh. Is there anything—"

The phone rang and she made a face, then picked up the receiver. "Fox & Fisher Detective Agency."

While he waited for her to finish with the call, he helped himself to the coffee. Every time he saw Nadine, she was busy. She wasn't the sort to sit around and wait for the work to come to her.

"I'll have Lindsay call with an update as soon as she can," Nadine said, scribbling a note on a message pad. She covered the mouthpiece for a moment. "Sorry, Jay. I'll be right with you."

When the call ended, she gave him a smile.

"You're good at multitasking," he observed.

"I love this job." She hesitated, then added, "Though, one day I would like to try my hand at the investigating side of the business. Lindsay and Nathan have given me a few small assignments." She sighed. "But I have a lot to learn before I'll be ready to take on a real case all by myself."

"You probably have as many qualifications as I do. Have you taken any courses?"

"Not yet. I'm signed up for six weeks of online instruction starting next month. Much to my mother's dismay."

"She doesn't like the idea of you being a private investigator?"

"Not hardly."

"Is she worried it's dangerous? Because according to Nathan, most of that exciting stuff only happens in the movies."

"It's partly a safety issue," she agreed. "But it's also an image thing. My mother, bless her dear, loving heart, is a bit of a snob."

The door opened, and Nathan came in just in time to hear Nadine's comment about her mother. "Hi, Nathan. How was the meeting?"

He had a briefcase in one hand and a cardboard box in the other, so Jay sprang forward to help him with the door. Nathan set the box on Nadine's desk, then hung his coat in the closet.

"The meeting went great. As you can see." He tapped the box. "We got the job. There are magazines in there that I'd like you to catalog for me please, Nadine."

He went to the coffeepot and filled one of the mugs.

"And you might as well come clean about your family. Jay's going to be part of the team soon, after all." He gave his friend a confident thumbs-up before disappearing into his office.

"Thanks, buddy." Jay wished he could be as sure of that. He turned and smiled at Nadine's obvious consternation. "So...what's this about your family?"

Her mouth twisted ruefully. "Just that we're rich and my cousin is sort-of famous. You'll understand when I tell you my real last name."

"It isn't Kimble?"

"I used my mother's surname when I applied for this job and it's sort of stuck. But my legal surname is Waverly."

He raised his eyebrows at a name he associated with a hotel chain and a blonde bombshell. "Are you related to Liz Waverly?"

"Yes. She's my cousin. As long as I keep my underwear on in public and don't put sex videos on the Internet, Dad's okay with this new career of mine. Mom, however, is still trying to adjust to the idea of me actually working for a living."

"But you must be beyond rich. Why *are* you working here?"

She leaned forward, her voice earnest. "Have you ever felt like you were born to do something?"

He thought of flying and the contradictory sensations of exhilaration and control. "Yes."

"Well, it may sound silly, but when I watched detective shows on TV as a kid, I knew that was what I wanted."

"Your family could buy you your own agency."

She shook her head. "This has to be something I earn. I need to work my way up the ladder."

"As a receptionist?"

"You have to start somewhere, and my fine arts degree wasn't much preparation for the real world. This is the first job I ever got on my own, with no help from my father. I'm learning the basics of the business, and one day—one day *soon*—I'll be ready for more."

Jay had liked Nadine from the first time he'd met her. Now he admired her grit. "I think you can do whatever you set your mind to."

"I'm banking on it." She tilted her head toward him. "Now what can I do to help you?"

Jay had to think for a moment to remember why he'd come out here in the first place. "Oh, yeah. I need to rent a car for tomorrow."

"A car. Really? You want to rent a car for tomorrow."

"Yeah, really." What was with her, anyway? It wasn't such a strange request.

"Okay, then." Nadine opened a neatly organized drawer and located a business card. "We have a corporate account with this company. I can make the booking for you."

Jay glanced down the hall. Kate hadn't budged since he'd left their office, but he'd hate for her to walk out at just the wrong moment and be tipped off about his plans.

"Thanks, but I'll call on my way to Eric's school. I have a meeting scheduled with his teacher, but I should be back in about an hour and a half."

"Okay."

Suddenly she wasn't meeting his eyes when she talked to him, but a minute ago she'd been completely at ease.

"What's up, Nadine?"

She just shook her head. "See you later, Jay. I hope the meeting with Eric's teacher goes well."

LINDSAY HAD SUGGESTED to Kate that they meet after work at the Stool Pigeon, to celebrate her first day at Fox & Fisher. At the last minute, though, she had to cancel because of a complication on one of her cases.

Kate decided to go on her own. Not that she particularly liked the place, but it was close and she wasn't keen to go home to her lonely apartment. The empty feeling wasn't because she missed Conner in particular—his betrayal seemed to have killed her feelings for him. She still hadn't cried over his fast exit from her life, and though he called her every night, she was never tempted to pick up the phone.

Still, she missed having company. She missed cooking for someone other than herself. And she wasn't all that fond of sleeping alone, either.

Wendy approached her table with a quizzical frown. "You okay? You don't look that great."

"I've got a cold," she finally admitted. She'd tried to fight it off, but she could no longer deny that she was under the weather. "Do you serve chicken soup?"

"Just clam chowder or French onion."

"I'll have the French onion," Kate decided. "Can you hold the melted cheese on top?"

"That's the best part, but sure. Anything else?"

"Green tea."

Wendy rolled her eyes. "How about regular tea?"

"I suppose."

Her order completed, Kate propped her elbows impolitely on the table and rested her chin on her palms. Maybe she should have gone home, after all. She really wasn't feeling well. After she ate, she'd splurge and take a cab rather than the subway.

As she contemplated the rest of her evening—maybe an hour watching *Prime Suspect,* then a hot bath—she noticed a tall man step into the pub. Even before he had looked in her direction, his powerful build and that imperturbable air of authority gave him away.

Captain Jay Savage was the sort of man strangers would turn to in a crisis. Kate could see heads turn in his direction, even now, as he hesitated over where to sit.

And then he spotted her.

For one electric moment she felt her pulse race, her skin grow hot. She put a hand to her cheek and wished she could blame her reaction on the bug she was fighting.

But, damn it, it was true. She found Jay Savage very attractive.

Not that she wanted to. She didn't want to be drawn to any man, let alone one who was competing for her job. Thankfully, she was well practiced in the art of concealing her emotions.

She took a deep breath as he made his way to her table and was perfectly calm by the time he asked, "Okay if I join you?"

"Why not?"

He settled into the booth seat without taking his eyes off her.

"Is something wrong?" she asked. "Do I have something on my face?"

"Your face is fine. It is a little flushed, though."

Because of him. No. She refused to admit it. "I've been fighting a cold."

"Well, that explains all the tissues you went through this afternoon. I thought maybe you had an allergy to my soap." He checked out the place with an uncertain expression. "Lindsay said the food here was good."

Kate shook her head. "You'll have to learn to discount Lindsay's opinion on matters of food and drink. Unless, of course, you're a fan of massive quantities of cholesterol and sugar."

"But she's so thin."

"Given her diet, it's one of the medical mysteries of the world."

"Well, I'm just here to kill time until my nephew's basketball practice is over. He's not that happy that I made him join the team so late in the season and I promised him we'd go out for pizza after. Speaking of weird diets…that kid could *live* on pepperoni and cheese."

"Why are you making him play basketball if he doesn't want to?"

"I'm worried about the trouble he could get into just hanging out with his buddies after school. I gave him his choice of activities. When he wouldn't commit to anything, I made a decision for him."

"Do you have reason to suspect he was getting into trouble?"

"Jeez, could you sound more like a cop?"

"It gets in your blood after a while."

He let out a jagged sigh. "We just had a meeting with his homeroom teacher this afternoon. He's been skipping a lot of classes this month and his grades are in free fall."

"Maybe he needs time off from his studies to deal with losing his mother."

"More free time is not a good idea for Eric, I'm afraid. The counselor I've spoken with suggested that a predictable routine would be the best thing."

"I see. How old is Eric?"

"He just turned fourteen."

"Was he having troubles at school before his mother passed away?"

"Probably, but I'm not sure." Jay rubbed a hand over his jaw. "I hadn't seen much of my sister and Eric the last few years. She started dating this guy… He was trouble, even worse than the usual losers she was attracted to. I guess I burned some bridges with her and I lost touch."

"You lost touch with Eric, as well?"

"I did, though I didn't mean to. A couple years can go by pretty fast when you're busy. But Eric sure changed a lot in those years. Now I know why my coworkers always complained when their kids hit the teenaged years."

"It must be difficult, suddenly finding yourself in the role of single parent."

"Especially since my sister had a heart of gold, but absolutely no sense of discipline. I've been letting Eric off easy, but the time has come to start setting down some rules."

"That's going to make you the bad guy."

"But it's got to be done. This is the age when his mother started getting into trouble. It began with boys, then skipping school, then alcohol and drugs. I do not want to go down that same road with Eric."

"Fourteen is a pivotal age for a boy," she agreed. "The basketball is probably a good idea."

"Yeah. The coach seems like a good guy. He did warn Eric that he expected hard work and lots of discipline."

"How does Eric feel about that?"

"I wish I had a clue. He's probably not impressed."

"You really have your hands full." Suddenly Kate felt guilty that she was trying to take a job away from a man who had to support his orphaned nephew. But surely Jay could find another job. This one had "Kate Cooper" stamped all over it.

When Wendy appeared with Kate's order, Jay asked for a glass of draft beer. Kate tucked into the soup, the warm broth soothing against her throat, the flavor rich and tasty.

After the first few spoonfuls, she became aware of Jay watching her. She paused with her spoon halfway to her mouth. "You're staring at me again."

"At least it isn't your legs this time." He realigned the cutlery on the table.

Her conscience compelled her to be honest with him. "Are you sure you want to be competing for this job?

Obviously your nephew needs a great deal of your time and energy right now."

"That's why I gave up flying, and I do need to make a living."

"But why with Fox & Fisher?" She set down her spoon. "No one could fault you for changing your mind. I know Nathan and Lindsay would completely understand. I have to tell you—I'm very close to solving this already."

She'd already tracked James Morgan to a lake resort three hours north of Manhattan. She had a car booked and planned to head out first thing in the morning, for a face-to-face interview. Potentially she could have everything wrapped up in the time it took to get a DNA sample back from the lab.

Poor Jay might well find this competition over before it even began.

"What's the matter, Kate? Afraid of a little competition?"

His tone was teasing, but she still felt annoyed.

Good lord, she'd been trying to be nice. He couldn't honestly believe he had any chance of finding Hannah's father before she did.

Well, she'd given him an opening to save face. Tomorrow he would find out, once and for all, that he was up against a professional.

WHEN KATE'S ALARM went off the following morning, every muscle in her body thought getting out of bed was a bad idea. She got up anyway. Today was the day she was going to end this charade of a competition between her and Jay Savage.

Once she'd had her shower she felt better. Facing her reflection as she dried her long curls into glossy submission, she thought with anticipation about the day ahead. It was always fun to get out of the city for a while, even in the winter, and she was looking forward to the drive to Liberty Lake.

She was also looking forward to seeing Jay Savage's face when she told him she had a sample of James Morgan's DNA at the lab for testing.

Kate took a vitamin pill with her orange juice, then loaded her leather bag with a packet of tissues, throat lozenges, hand disinfectant and pain tablets, just so she would be prepared.

A delay on the subway had her arriving at the car agency fifteen minutes later than she'd planned. She pushed through the glass door with one hand, while at the same time searching her bag for her notebook which contained her reservation confirmation number.

"Fancy meeting you here."

Her hand froze in the purse. By now she knew that voice all too well. She looked up. Jay Savage was dangling a set of keys in front of her. The man looked hale and hearty, in a sheepskin-lined leather jacket ideal for a day in the country. But he couldn't possibly be headed for the same place she was.

"You aren't planning to go to Liberty Lake by any chance?" he asked.

He was. How had he managed to trump her again?

"Obviously you weren't as preoccupied with your nephew's problems as I thought."

His pleased smile waned. "I'm doing everything I can to help Eric. And that includes finding a new career."

Again, she felt that pinprick of guilt, knowing that he needed this job not only for himself, but for his nephew, too.

He could find something else, she reminded herself. *This is my job. Lindsay promised it to me first.*

Trying to disguise her chagrin, she shrugged. "Great. Well, if you'll excuse me, I have a car to pick up." She tried to step around him to the counter, but he touched her arm.

"It doesn't make sense for us to both rent a car and drive all that way. Why don't I just fill you in when I return?"

"Good idea. Only I'll fill *you* in when *I* return." She tried again to get around him, but once more he blocked her.

"We'll both go," he said.

She sighed. "All right."

"In the same car."

She hesitated, torn between his practical proposition and her personal preference to make the trip alone. Maybe, if she got to Liberty Lake first, she could still scoop him on the DNA sample.

Brilliant idea, Kate. What are you now? A rally driver? Much as she hated to admit it, his idea was the most logical.

"Okay, fine," she said. "We'll take the same car. But come back to the counter. I want my name listed in the contract as one of the drivers. And I'm taking the first shift behind the wheel."

CHAPTER SIX

KATE DIDN'T LOOK WELL, but Jay hesitated to say anything. He didn't often run across people with a stronger competitive urge than his, but he suspected Kate fell in that category. She'd sooner expire from exhaustion than admit she wasn't up to driving.

Not that he felt unsafe. She was keeping her attention on the road and maintaining a reasonable speed. But her face was flushed and she was going through throat drops like candy.

"How's the gas?" he asked, thinking if they stopped at a station, he'd be able to suggest it was his turn to drive.

"Almost full."

Damn compact cars. They should have rented a gas-guzzling SUV. Jay gazed out the window at the forested hills sprawled on either side of the highway. They'd left urban life behind about an hour ago. According to his GPS they still had almost two hours to go.

Kate reached for the cup holder and took a swig of the orange juice she'd brought along for the trip. Then she popped another throat drop.

"Are you sure you're feeling okay?"

"I'm fine," she insisted, her tone edgy.

She didn't look fine. A sheen of sweat had formed on her brow. "Well, I'm sure you wouldn't risk our lives by driving when you knew you weren't up to it."

She glared at him, but otherwise made no reply.

Interesting woman. He wondered if she would ever reveal her softer side to him. Maybe she didn't have one. But then he supposed if you wanted to work for the NYPD, you had to be tough.

Kate certainly acted like she was.

She didn't look it, though, and maybe that was why she adopted an extra edge when she was working. In profile her features were delicate, and her hands on the steering wheel were fine-boned and elegant, despite the closely cropped fingernails that spoke to her practical nature. She was a very thin woman, especially in her upper body, with a narrow rib cage and high, small breasts. He'd bet she was hot in a bikini. And even hotter without one.

"You've got to stop looking at me like that."

Her glare made him smile. "How did you know how I was looking at you?" He could have sworn she was concentrating on the road.

"I've worked with male partners ever since I graduated from the academy. Trust me, I know."

"Is that why you're so serious around me? Are you afraid I'll hit on you?"

"Why? Do you want to?"

The direct challenge caught him by surprise. He found himself thinking it over. *Did* he want to? His body immediately reacted to the idea, which was an answer he wasn't about to share with Kate.

"You're a very attractive woman—"

"Oh, forget it. I was just yanking your chain. The reason I'm serious around you is because whenever you see me, I'm at work, and I take my work very seriously. It's why I'm eventually going to win this competition and get this job."

"If this guy at Liberty Lake turns out to be our man, you won't win. We'll be tied."

She scowled. "Don't I know it."

"Maybe they'll give us a second case to work on."

For a moment he thought she was going to explode. Then he realized she was laughing, and he joined in. Enjoying the release of tension, Jay confided, "I'm serious about my work, too. Believe me, you wouldn't want to fly with a pilot who wasn't."

She flashed her gray-green eyes in his direction, her gaze curious. "How old were you when you decided you wanted to fly for a living?"

"Oh, I was young. Like a lot of kids, I was fascinated by planes. When I was about six we lived very close to the airport. I used to hike to a field beside the flight path. I'd lie in the grass and watch the planes soar over my head."

He used to wonder where all the people were going. One day, he promised himself, he'd go places, too. And not just as a passenger.

"Your mom let you do that by yourself?"

"She wasn't what you'd call a 'hands-on' kind of

parent. She had a lot on her mind. Most of the time I had my kid sister with me. She liked planes, too."

Until she was older. Then she'd started liking boys. And alcohol. And, for a brief period of time, drugs. For years he'd tried to figure out what he could have done to help Tracy turn out differently. He'd never found any answers. Which didn't bode well for Eric, he was afraid.

"What about your dad?"

"He was with the army. The year Tracy was born he was killed in Nicaragua."

Maybe life had been good before then. Jay had no way of knowing for sure, though there were photos that suggested his mother had once been not only kind and loving, but also sober.

"That must have been tough."

"We survived." He had, anyway. His mother had died well before her time. And now Tracy was gone, too. They had both died from overdoses of the substances they were addicted to. And he had stood helplessly on the sidelines watching it happen.

Now his nephew faced the same dangers. Drugs or gangs. Either one could kill him. But how could he convince the fourteen-year-old that he was on the wrong path?

He twisted slightly in his seat. Time was ticking away, along with the miles. Since they'd started talking, Kate didn't seem to be reaching for as many of her cough candies. Maybe the conversation was distracting her. Or perhaps the little white pill she'd swallowed earlier was finally taking effect.

At any rate, he'd rather chat than sit in silence and stew about his problems. "What about you? Where did you grow up?"

"In Manhattan. The Upper East Side. My parents both taught at State University."

"Any brothers or sisters?"

She gave him a dour look. "My parents were in their forties when I was born, and not about to make the same mistake twice. Dad got snipped before I was even born."

"I suppose that was the smart thing to do, if he knew he didn't want more kids. I hear it's a simple operation, as surgeries go."

She seemed surprised he had said that. "Out of curiosity…how would you know?"

He shrugged. For years he'd been toying with the idea of getting a vasectomy. Unplanned pregnancy was a sort of theme with his family. First his mother, then his sister. He was always very careful with birth control, but it would be nice to know that he was one hundred percent safe.

"You don't want to have kids?" she pressed.

"No." He'd spent his childhood raising his sister. Now he had Eric to worry about. "Do you?"

Her answer surprised the hell out of him.

"More than anything."

AN HOUR LATER, Kate spotted the turnoff for Liberty Lake. A narrow paved road led fifteen miles off the highway to a lake nestled in the midst of a heavily treed valley. The road stopped about two hundred yards shy of the beach. The lake would be frozen at this time of year and the sand was covered with snow, but Kate could tell it would be heavenly in the summer. A row of cabins stood behind a tall stand of spruce. Only one cottage, bigger than the rest, had been built along the shoreline.

"Nice place." Jay had been quiet ever since she'd admitted how badly she wanted children. She wondered what had shocked him so much.

Did he think that someone who had worked as a police officer couldn't be a good mother?

Or did he simply find the idea of wanting children incomprehensible?

She thought about Conner, who had told her he'd like to have three or four children, too. When he'd told her that, she'd felt so sure that they were made for one another. But maybe he'd only been saying what he thought she wanted to hear.

Last night was the first time he hadn't tried to call her since she'd moved him out of her apartment. She wondered if he'd already moved on. Maybe he was more serious about Emily White than she'd thought.

Whatever the reason, she really didn't care.

Again, she felt fortunate that she'd discovered the truth about his character before the wedding and not after.

"There's a sign for visitor parking." Jay pointed out a right-hand turn, and she coasted the small car into a slot in a row of empty parking spaces.

Kate squirted some disinfectant hand-wash into her palm and rubbed it over her hands. Then she pulled a wool hat over her head and stepped out into the gray, cold day, her feet settling on packed snow. All the cabins appeared vacant—which was to be expected given this was off-season.

Still, Kate had no trouble imagining what the resort would be like in the summer. The green of the trees, the smell of the water, the sound of children laughing and splashing. All of the happiest times of her childhood had been spent at a summer camp in a setting much like this one.

At camp her parents' opinions hadn't mattered so much. The physical activities she loved—swimming, softball, running—were actually encouraged and there were no white linens to worry about at meal times.

"I guess the owners must live in the big house on the lake," Jay said.

Kate agreed, and set out with him in that direction. A path had been shoveled through the snow and they followed this until the sound of voices diverted their attention to the lake. A man and a woman were out on snowshoes, heading toward the cottage. Wooden steps leading from the cottage to the lake had been cleared of snow and she and Jay waited there as the couple approached.

"Are you looking for us?" the man asked as he drew near. He was about five foot nine, in his mid-forties, trim and obviously in good shape. The woman beside him seemed similar in age, a few inches shorter, with the sort of pale skin that turned brilliant red when cold—much like Kate's.

"That depends," Kate replied. "Are you James Morgan?"

"Sure am, though I usually go by Jimmy. This is my wife, Samantha."

"Sammy," the woman corrected with a smile.

Jimmy and Sammy. Too cute. Kate couldn't hold it against them, though. There was something inherently likable about these people, who, judging from their friendly behavior, were not the sort to fear bad news from strangers.

"I'm Kate Cooper and this is Jay Savage. We're private investigators with a firm in New York City. We've been hired by Hannah Young to locate her biological father."

"And you figure I can help you find him?"

"Do you remember Rebecca Wagner?" she asked, using Rebecca's maiden name.

Jimmy went still. Then he swallowed. "I think we better go to the house and pour some drinks."

As she followed the Morgans up a set of stairs, through a porch and into a large, open family room, Kate felt she was entering a home filled with comfort and love. The cottage had white wainscoting on the walls and wide windows overlooking the lake. The decorating was haphazard, everything from the furniture to the knick-knacks to the paintings on the walls had been chosen with no particular theme in mind, and nothing in the room seemed to have been purchased in the current decade.

Still, the ultimate effect was to make a guest sigh and feel at ease.

Jimmy went to a cabinet and took down a bottle of port. Kate and Jay both declined, but Sammy accepted a small glass and immediately swallowed all of it.

"Rebecca is the girl I told you about in my first year of college," Jimmy told his wife. "She dropped out of school before finals. I never thought to wonder why. We hadn't, um, gone out again after that first time." He turned to Kate. "I take it she had a child?"

Kate glanced at Jay. He was following the conversation with interest, but didn't seem annoyed that she'd taken the lead with the questioning. She turned back to Jimmy. "Yes. She had a daughter."

Jimmy gave a long whistle of amazement. His wife stepped behind him and put her hand on his shoulder. He rested his own hand over hers. A nice gesture of solidarity, Kate thought.

"Hannah Young, you said?" Jimmy sought confirmation in her eyes and Kate nodded.

"If she was conceived in your first year of college, she must be about twenty-five," Samantha calculated.

"Wow." Jimmy gave a slight shake of his head. "This is amazing." He turned to his wife. "Samantha and I— we weren't able to have children. We've come to terms with that and we have a great life. But, why did Rebecca wait so long to tell me?"

"Rebecca gave her daughter up for adoption," Kate explained. "Hannah has been very happy with her adoptive parents and the only reason she wants to find her birth parents now is to make sure there are no genetic problems in her family tree. She recently married and she and her husband are hoping to have children."

"Wow," Jimmy said again. "Well, you can tell her not to worry on my account. My parents are alive and healthy and both sets of grandparents are still around, as well. I'd love to meet her and so would they, I'm sure."

"It's not that simple," Jay cautioned.

At Jimmy's and Samantha's confused frowns, Kate said, "Rebecca isn't certain who the father is. She has given us the names of three possibilities, one of whom is you. Only DNA testing will give us the definitive answer Hannah needs."

"Three possibilities," Samantha said, her tone a little incredulous.

"That doesn't sound good, but Rebecca was a nice kid from a strict family," Jimmy explained to his wife. "A lot of us went a little wild with our first taste of freedom."

Kate thought it was gallant that he was so quick to defend Rebecca. Apparently so did his wife. She smiled gently. "Wild? You, Jimmy?"

He laughed, then poured a second helping of the port for both of them. "I guess I had my moments."

They were such a sweet couple. And what a gene pool. Kate really hoped that Jimmy would turn out to be Hannah's father.

"So how do we test my DNA?" Jimmy asked. "Do I need to go to a doctor or something?"

"Actually, it's very easy." Kate opened her leather bag and extracted the kit she'd brought from the office. "We just need a swab of saliva from your mouth, then we send it, along with a sample from Hannah and Rebecca, to the lab."

Jimmy cast his wife a nervous glance. "That is easy. How long until we'll know the results?"

"The agency uses an express service, so it takes only two working days. And the results are virtually one hundred percent accurate."

"Oh my God." The enormity of it all was finally sinking in. Jimmy sagged down on a kitchen stool. "I could have a *daughter*. A twenty-five-year-old daughter."

"And perhaps, in nine months or so, a grandchild," added his wife.

He locked gazes with her, and slowly they both smiled.

Kate's eyes watered as she watched the slow blossoming of an abandoned dream. They hadn't been able to have children of their own. It would be such a wonderful gift if Jimmy turned out to be Hannah's father. As she reached for a tissue, she noticed Jay watching her.

"This darn cold," she muttered.

CHAPTER SEVEN

AFTER THEIR MEETING with the Morgans was concluded, Kate and Jay headed back to the rental car. Kate's head was pounding now and she felt so chilled she could hardly wait to get into the car and crank up the heat.

"My turn to drive," Jay said.

She didn't have the energy to argue. She placed her bag with the DNA sample in the backseat, then relinquished the car keys to him.

She sank into her seat and barely managed to find the energy to fasten her seat belt. God, it felt good to relax.

Jay backed out of the parking space and started along the road toward the highway. She waited impatiently for the vehicle to warm up, but even fifteen minutes later she still felt cold.

"Mind if I turn up the heat?"

"It's already—" Jay looked at her assessingly, then acquiesced. "Sure. Go ahead."

She adjusted the dials and a moment later, hot air was blowing at her feet, slowly warming her from the bottom up.

She needed another pain reliever, preferably two, but

the vial was somewhere in the bottom of her leather bag and she felt too tired to search for it. She hated feeling under the weather like this. What she needed was a good night's sleep. The idea of sinking under her down comforter was heaven, but first she'd need to take the DNA samples to Nadine and make sure they were sent by rush courier to the lab.

She couldn't leave that job to Jay, because technically, if he was the one who sent in the sample, then he would be able to say he solved the case, which was so far from the truth.

Well, maybe not that far from the truth. He wasn't as bad at this job as she'd expected he would be. In fact, he was aggravatingly clever…getting that appointment with Rebecca before her, then tracking down Morgan just as quickly as she had.

She turned her head slightly and studied his profile. He'd slipped on a pair of aviator sunglasses that only made him look more like the captain of a big airliner.

"Driving a car must be boring compared to flying a plane."

"Not even comparable."

"Tell me about flying. How does it work?"

"You really want to know?"

She nodded.

"Okay. You need to understand two sets of related concepts. The first is drag and thrust. The second is gravity and lift."

"Drag and thrust, gravity and lift," she repeated.

He nodded. "When thrust—from the power of the engines and propellers—overcomes drag, or air resistance, the plane moves forward. When lift—from low pressure created on the top of the wing—overcomes gravity, the plane rises in the air."

"It's that simple, huh?"

"I can make it a lot more complicated if you like." He grinned.

"No thanks. You could talk about the concepts for an hour and flying would still seem like magic to me."

"You're right about that. I've spent years learning the science behind aviation, but when you see the sun setting from six miles above the earth, well, it's an experience you never forget."

"You'll go back to flying one day," she guessed.

He nodded. "That's the plan. When, or should I say *if,* Eric finishes high school."

"When will that be—another four years?"

He nodded.

"I know it will end us in stalemate, but I sure hope Jimmy turns out to be Hannah's dad."

"No health issues with him," Jay agreed. "Plus he seemed like a genuinely nice guy. I don't think I'd have reacted as agreeably if I suddenly found out I had a twenty-five-year-old kid."

"But then you don't want to have children."

"That's right," he confirmed.

She waited for him to say more, but he didn't. "How can you be so certain?"

"I don't have kids right now and I'm happy with that.

I think it's more puzzling how you can be so sure you'll want children when you don't have any. As an only child, you never even had to babysit siblings."

"Maybe I didn't have brothers or sisters, but I was a camp counselor in the summer. I worked with kids of all ages. And loved it."

"Really? See, I would hate a job like that."

"Maybe you'd surprise yourself."

"I doubt it."

She still wasn't satisfied. "What if you fall in love with someone who wants a family? What will you do then?"

"I'm thirty-three years old, I've dated a lot of women, and it hasn't happened yet." He smiled. "I think the women who want husbands and kids and picket fences spot me a mile away and go running."

"Sorry. I forgot. A different woman in every city. I hope you're honest with them, at least."

His smile faded. "What's that supposed to mean?"

"Just that if you're not in an exclusive relationship with someone it's important to be up-front about that."

He glanced at her, eyes narrowed. "Are we talking about me now? Or your ex?"

Touché. She *had* been thinking of Conner.

"So he cheated on you, huh?"

She nodded.

"Don't tar me with that brush," Jay said. "I don't date more than one woman at a time. And I'm always extremely honest. I'm sorry the man that you were with wasn't the same."

THE CAR WAS SO HOT, Jay could hardly breathe, but he wasn't about to turn down the heat because Kate had finally stopped shivering.

"I'm sorry for judging your lifestyle," Kate said. "I'm just embarrassed it took me so long to catch on that my fiancé was a liar and a cheat."

"People always say that. But it's human nature to trust the ones we love."

"Well, burned once, second time shy, right? I can really relate to that old saying now."

When he'd first met her, he'd found her cold, focused, all business. But he'd seen her tear up in front of the Morgans. She had a soft side, all right.

"You feel like you won't love again, ever. But, Kate, I can tell that you will."

She crossed her arms over her chest, clearly not convinced.

"How else will you have that big family you want so much?"

"There are ways."

Traffic was getting heavier now that he was nearing the city and he didn't dare look too closely into her eyes. "You mean going to one of those clinics for donor sperm?"

"That's one option."

"You can't be serious."

"I'm thirty-two years old. If I want to have four children before I'm forty, and if I want to space them a few years apart, then I really don't have much time."

"You've got this all planned out, don't you?"

She sighed. "Ever hear about the biological clock?

Men don't have to worry about that, but women are forced to be realistic."

"Fair enough." He passed a lineup of three semitrailers, then switched back into the right-hand lane. "But there must be other options to artificial insemination."

"Such as?"

"Well…" He hesitated. What were the other options? "Adoption?"

"Possibly."

"Or—" A Lamborghini rushed by on his left with a speed that rocked the compact Subaru. "You could always ask a friend…"

"You think?"

"Why not?"

"What if one of your female friends asked you for a favor like that? How would you react?"

Something inside of him shriveled at the prospect. "I don't know."

She saw right through him. "You'd say no."

"Probably," he conceded.

She gazed despondently out the window. "I think most guys would."

If they had any sense they would. But if they understood how much their friend wanted children, and if they were convinced she would make a good mother…

Jay gave his head a thorough, mental shake. What the hell was he thinking? They weren't talking about him here. This was some theoretical guy.

Not that making love with Kate wasn't a tempting proposition.

FOR THE LAST HOUR of the trip, Kate napped and Jay tried to keep his thoughts focused on the sorts of things he *ought* to be concerned about—his driving, the case, what to do about Eric—and not on the things he *shouldn't* be thinking about—the way Kate had cried at the Morgans', the hurt look in her eyes whenever she spoke about her ex-fiancé, the way her face shone when she mentioned having babies.

They were already in Manhattan when Kate woke up.

"Sorry. I must have dozed."

"You obviously needed the rest. How are you feeling?"

"Better," she said as she reached into her bag for another lozenge.

Yeah, right.

Kate popped the lozenge in her mouth. "I was thinking we should take Jimmy's DNA sample straight to the BioFinds Lab. We have about an hour before it closes. That way we'll get the results even faster. Then we can return the rental car."

"Since you're obviously not feeling well, why don't I drop you home first? Then I can take the sample to the lab and return the car."

"Oh, sure. And technically you would have solved the case."

"I wouldn't pull a stunt like that."

She looked at him closely. "No. I guess you wouldn't. But I'll be fine for another hour or so."

"If you insist." He'd just been trying to be considerate. But he had to admit he didn't mind having her company a little longer.

When he pulled up to the laboratory twenty minutes later, Kate suggested he drop her off outside the building and wait in the car.

"We've come this far together, we might as well see it through." He circled around to a parking space, then pulled off his sunglasses and smiled. "Not that I don't trust you."

She had the good grace to look embarrassed.

He was standing beside her when she handed over the sample and he watched as she wrote down The Fox & Fisher Detective Agency address on the form. By the time they were back in the car, he could tell her energy was lagging.

This time when he suggested driving her home, she agreed.

"I'd appreciate that."

The fact that she acquiesced so easily told him how badly she must be feeling. He followed her directions to an apartment not that far from his own, just a block off Riverside Park. He lucked into a parking spot in front of the three-story building.

Kate seemed unsteady as she got out of the car, and he went around to the passenger side to help her.

"I'm fine," she insisted, but when he put an arm around her waist, she didn't resist.

He stayed by her side until they were inside the walk-up, in the first-level hallway next to a door numbered 104. As they unlocked the dead bolt—Kate locating the right key on the ring, then passing it to him—a thin, attractive woman in her forties passed by. She looked at Jay, then at Kate, and raised her eyebrows.

Kate managed a faint smile. "Hi, Janet. This is Jay Savage. We're working together."

"That's nice." Kate's neighbor smiled, then continued on her way.

"I don't think she believed you."

"I think she's just glad I'm not with Conner anymore. She's the one who told me about the affair."

After opening the door, he passed her back the keys. "You're sure you'll be okay?"

"Absolutely." She tossed her coat and bag on the floor, and tried to kick off her boots. When she stumbled, Jay reached for her.

"Man, you're stubborn." Keeping one arm around her, he used the other hand to pull off first one boot, then the other. "Why can't you just admit you're sick?"

"I don't believe in getting sick. I don't have time for it."

Beyond her determined expression, he saw exhaustion—both physical and emotional. She'd been through a lot lately, first the breakup of her relationship, then quitting her job, and now this competition of theirs.

"I think I had the same bug the week after Tracy died. If you feel anything like I did then, I can't believe you're still standing."

"I probably wouldn't be if you weren't holding me up," she admitted.

The color of her eyes was changeable, and now they seemed vividly green against her flushed cheeks.

His first impression of her had been that she was

tough and smart and formidable, but suddenly she seemed the opposite of all those things—vulnerable, sweet and defenseless.

He put a hand to her forehead. Her skin was soft, but also hot. "You've got a fever."

She dropped her gaze. "I just need a good night's sleep."

"That would be a start," he agreed. "Which way to the bedroom?"

"Hey…we haven't even had our first date yet."

It was just a joke, but he was surprised at the instant stab of yearning he felt. "Very funny, Kate. You're off men at the present, remember?"

He glanced around, trying to figure out which way to go. There was a galley kitchen to the right—well used, judging from the open shelves displaying jars of pasta, flour and rice, and a collection of aged copper pots.

In the other direction a short hall led past a charming living room, decorated in warm blues and golds with nothing breakable or fussy. It was the sort of home where he could imagine children growing up healthy, loved and well cared for.

Not that it would be big enough for the four children Kate planned on having.

With his arm still around her, he headed down the hall. The master bedroom was small, even by New York standards. Basically all that fit inside was a bureau and a queen-size bed.

As soon as she saw it, Kate toppled on top of the fluffy, patchwork quilt. "Oh, God, it feels good to get my feet up. You've been so kind. Thank you. I hope I don't repay you by passing this bug on."

"Like I said, I think I've already had it." He hung back at the door, knowing he should get going, yet reluctant to do it. "You'd be more comfortable if you changed into pajamas."

"I will. Later."

"And you should take something for that fever."

She opened the drawer of her night table and pulled out a vial of Tylenol. He watched as she swallowed two tablets, and saw her grimace as they went down.

He bet her throat was sore. Without asking her, because he was sure she would say no, he went to the kitchen and made her a cup of tea. He found the fridge and cupboards well stocked, so he put lemon and honey in the tea, and some biscuits on a small plate, as well.

Her eyes rounded with surprise when he placed the plate and cup on her bedside table. "You didn't have to go to all that trouble. It's after six. Shouldn't you be getting home to your nephew?"

"Yes, but I'd feel better leaving if there was someone here to take care of you."

She laughed. "I'm a big girl. And this is just a cold. I'll be fine."

"Okay. Hope you feel better." As he turned to leave, he noticed a frame facedown on her bureau. "Mind if I look at this?"

She sighed. "Go ahead."

Kate smiled up at him, beautiful and happy beside a man who looked utterly pleased with himself. Jay disliked her ex-fiancé on sight, though he could see that the man was handsome in a chiseled-features sort of way. He placed the frame back as he'd found it.

"You're sure you're okay?"

"All I need is sleep, which I can't do with you standing there watching me."

"I suppose that was your sweet way of thanking me for my concern?"

"Sorry, but I don't do sweet."

He noticed a framed piece of embroidery on the wall. A picture of a kitten on a rocking chair next to a fireplace. Home Sweet Home was embroidered along the bottom of the picture, along with the initials *K.L.C.*

She didn't do sweet. Right.

CHAPTER EIGHT

JAY PICKED UP A ROTISSERIE chicken, some buns and a bag of washed lettuce on his way home. Eric was already in the apartment, watching TV. With his hat off, his angelic blond curls softened the adolescent gawkiness of his face and Jay was reminded of the little boy who had been so easy to get along with.

"Hey there, Eric. Sorry I'm late…but I've got dinner ready to go."

All he received for a reply was a grunt.

"It isn't much." Jay set the groceries out on the table, along with a bottle of salad dressing. "But I figure we have the major food groups covered."

He poured two glasses of milk, then glanced into the living room. When food was involved, Eric wasn't usually shy. "You hungry?"

Eric ambled into the kitchen and looked over the hastily assembled meal with disinterest.

Jay vowed to make more of an effort tomorrow night. They'd been doing too much of the last-minute, pick-up sort of food lately. "On the weekend I'll buy some steak," he offered. "We can bake potatoes and real vegetables to go with it."

Eric didn't seem interested in menu planning with him. He put a little food on his plate, then started toward the living room.

"Let's eat at the table for a change."

"Why?"

"I figure it's time we settled into a regular routine."

"Why can't our routine be eating in the living room?"

Jay twisted the cap off the bottle of Italian dressing. "Because we need to touch base at some point in the day. Might as well be over dinner."

Eric didn't look impressed with that argument, but he sat down. Head bent over his plate, he started to eat.

"Did the coach give you a copy of the basketball schedule yet?"

Eric went to the backpack he'd left lying on the floor by the front door, rustled around a bit, then pulled out a sheet of paper. "Here."

Jay smoothed out the wrinkles so he could read it. Between practices and games, it seemed Eric would be busy after school every day but Tuesday and Thursday.

"You know how your teacher suggested we hire a tutor to help you catch up with your classes?"

Big sigh. "Yeah."

"I tried calling a couple names on the list she gave us. One of them is a first-year math major named Kevin Hodges. What do you say we give him a try? He said he'd meet you at the library after your last class."

Eric shrugged.

"I was thinking two times a week to start."

"Why *two* times? Once is more than enough."

"When you get your grades up a little we can talk about cutting back."

"What if I can't get my grades up? Maybe I'm not smart like you."

"You're capable of passing high school. That's all I'm asking. Whether you do better than that is up to you. When I was a kid, I was motivated. I wanted to be a pilot, and I knew the competition was going to be tough. You need to find something that motivates *you*."

"Maybe nothing motivates me."

Jay couldn't help but think of Tracy and all the times he'd tried to help her with her homework, to no avail. She'd only laughed at him. She simply hadn't cared.

"A good education can make all the difference in your life, Eric. That, and staying away from the wrong kind of friends…and alcohol and drugs."

That was their unfortunate family legacy. But he'd do everything he could to save his nephew from that fate.

Eric ate another mouthful, then took his plate to the trash can. Jay had his back to him, but he could hear the food being scraped into the garbage. It frustrated him having good food going to waste. "Is that all you're eating?"

"I'm not hungry. Can I watch TV now?" he asked, his voice full of grievance.

He supposed Eric had loaded up on junk food after school. "In a few minutes. We haven't done talking. Now that we're living together, we need to divvy up the chores. What jobs did you used to do when it was you and your mom?"

Eric looked at him incredulously. "I didn't have chores. I didn't have a curfew, either."

"I know it's different living with me."

"Isn't that the truth."

Jay did his best to ignore the resentment in Eric's voice. "And I'm sure you must miss your mom very much."

"Oh, sure. I really miss coming home to find her passed out on the living room couch. But at least I had some freedom then. She didn't make me go to basketball, and have meetings with my teachers and sit down at the table to eat. This is all crap." Eric pushed a chair out of his way, then left the room.

The grating sound of metal legs against tile flooring rang in Jay's ears for the next few minutes. The comment about Tracy's drinking stung. Though he knew it was true, he also knew that Eric had loved his mother.

What the hell should he do now? Go talk to Eric?

Maybe he ought to give him a chance to cool off.

He stared at the food he no longer had any appetite for. How in the hell were the two of them going to survive the next four years together?

"KATE? MAY I INTERRUPT you for a moment?"

Kate couldn't imagine anyone saying no to Nadine. The receptionist was just too genuine and lovely. It was hard to believe that she was a Waverly heiress, but Lindsay had assured her that this was the case. And she certainly did dress the part. Today she was wearing an elegant black cashmere dress, tights and patent leather boots.

"What's up, Nadine?"

The petite woman was carrying a mug which she now handed to Kate. "Are you feeling better? I made you a special tea. It's supposed to boost your immune system."

"Thank you. I am feeling a lot better. I had a really good sleep last night."

She was relieved she had bounced back so quickly. Jay had proven to be a worthy adversary and she didn't want to risk falling behind.

"I hope you don't mind," Nadine said, "but I'm so curious. What happened yesterday? Both you and Jay asked me about rental cars. Were you going to the same place?"

Kate rolled her eyes. "Yes. We didn't know that, though, until we ran into each other at the rental shop. We ended up driving in one vehicle to save the firm on expenses."

"Nathan will appreciate that." She lowered her voice, and a gleam brightened her eyes. "So you spent the day with Jay. What was that like? He looks like he should be starring in action-adventure movies in the Amazon, not walking around Manhattan like a normal guy. Is he as amazing as he seems?"

Nadine had quite the active imagination. Still, Kate had to admit her casting was quite accurate. Jay did have the combination of masculine strength and unexpected tenderness that made for a compelling action hero.

He'd been so gallant last night, too, helping her home and making sure she was all right. Totally unnecessary, of course, but a part of her had reveled in the attention.

She couldn't remember anyone fussing over her in that way before. Not her parents. And not Conner, either.

Her most vivid recollection was the way Jay had touched her forehead. She'd relived that moment many times over since then. The gentle contact had been unexpectedly sweet, but also surprisingly erotic….

"Oh, you're blushing. I'm sorry if I said the wrong thing. But this competition is so exciting. I wonder if this is what it's like at the CIA? You know, everything is top secret and you have to be careful you don't tell the wrong person the wrong thing."

"You're really in the middle here, aren't you?"

Nadine nodded. "It's killing me. Especially since I wish both you and Jay could win."

"Well, hopefully this competition will be over soon. I'm getting close to tracking down the other two prospective fathers."

Nadine edged forward on her chair. "In confidence, do you mind telling me your strategy? I'm hoping to be an investigator, too, one day, and I'm trying to learn as I go. I typed all the reports so I know there are three possible fathers. But when it comes to locating them… where on earth do you start?"

Kate didn't mind answering Nadine's questions. The receptionist's enthusiasm was contagious. Besides, it gave her the perfect opportunity to organize her own thoughts on the subject.

First she gave Nadine a quick rundown of how she—and to be fair, Jay, too—had located James Morgan. "He turned out to be a wonderful man with a really sweet wife. They don't have children and I think it would be such an unexpected gift for them if Hannah turns out to be James's daughter."

Nadine pressed her hands together. "I hope he's the one."

"We'll soon know. Jay and I dropped the DNA samples at the lab last night. The results should be here within two business days, as long as there are no delays. I can just imagine how anxious Jimmy and his wife must be feeling."

"Did he look anything like Hannah?"

Kate had looked for a resemblance yesterday and still wasn't sure if she'd spotted one. "A little around the eyes, maybe."

"That's good. But you must think there's a chance he isn't her father, or you wouldn't be trying to find the other two men."

"To be frank, if Jay wasn't hot on my heels, I would probably wait for the test results before proceeding," Kate admitted. She'd underestimated Jay before, though, and had almost lost as a result.

"So what's your next step?"

"I know prospective dad two and three went to New England College twenty-five years ago. According to the college database, they both graduated four years later."

She opened two screens on her computer and arranged them side by side. She beckoned Nadine to come and stand beside her so she could have a better view of the notes she'd compiled for each of the men.

She pointed the cursor to the file on the left which

had prospective dad two's name followed by all the information she knew about him. "Gary Gifford graduated with an education degree, specializing in physical education. He played on the college football team for all four years as quarterback."

"A jock," Nadine surmised. "Hannah doesn't look like the athletic type to me. Not that that proves anything," she added hastily.

"But it's an interesting detail to notice," Kate encouraged her. "Oliver Crane, on the other hand, was a total academic. He was on the debating team and graduated with a political science degree, which suggested to me that he might have applied for law school."

"It's a common career path," Nadine agreed. "A couple of my friends are doing just that."

Kate nodded. "It becomes a game of methodical searching after that. In this case, I was lucky. Oliver didn't leave the state to get his law degree and I found him on the graduating roster of New York University in 1990."

Nadine looked impressed. "So what do you do now?"

"There are so many possibilities, the head spins. But I like to start with the most logical and assume that he's practicing law somewhere in Manhattan. I hope to find out for certain by checking the bar association membership listing."

"Lindsay's sister is a lawyer," Nadine offered. "Maybe she can help you find him." She covered her mouth. "Oops. Lindsay warned me not to help one of you more than the other."

Kate smiled. Nadine's transparent honesty was one

of her most likable qualities, but it wouldn't necessarily be an asset if she was serious about a career as an investigator.

"Don't worry. I've met Meg before and I've already set up a meeting with her for eleven o'clock. Do you think we could use the conference room?"

"I'll make sure it's available." Nadine leaned closer to the computer screen, scanning some of the other data Lindsay had gathered about each of the men. "You've checked so many databases. Are they all easily available?"

"Not as much to an investigator as they are to a cop, unfortunately." In some respects, working privately was like having one arm tied behind her back. "But if it was easy, our clients wouldn't need to hire us, would they?"

JAY WASN'T SURPRISED to find Kate in their office when he arrived at work late that morning. A virus—no matter how virulent—wouldn't keep her down for long.

"You look better," he commented as he set his briefcase on his makeshift desk.

"I think I kicked the bug. Thanks again for seeing me home yesterday. That was above and beyond."

"It was nothing."

"Maybe to you. I've never had someone bring me a cup of tea in bed before."

"Never?" He found that very hard to believe. "Not even your mother?" His mother had been largely absent, but even so, he could remember her fussing when he was genuinely ill.

"I wasn't a complainer."

"Stalwart even as a child?"

"I guess it was a defense mechanism. My way of coping with the realization that my parents were largely indifferent to my existence."

Jay would have thought she was angling for sympathy, but her tone was matter-of-fact.

"Don't get me wrong," she added. "My parents were never mean or cruel. They bought me everything I needed, kept me fed and clothed…you know, the basics."

Love ought to be considered one of the basics, Jay thought. Lord knew, he loved Eric. But these days he didn't know how to show it. Eric had been silent and sullen this morning and though he'd left for school, Jay had no idea if he actually intended to go to his classes.

He rubbed his chin and sighed.

"More trouble with Eric?" Kate guessed.

He nodded. But before he could unload any of his worries, Nadine was at the door, motioning to Kate.

"Meg's here for her appointment. She's waiting in the conference room."

As Kate exited, he was left wondering what she was up to now. Had she found out something about one of the two other prospective fathers?

LINDSAY WAS CHATTING with her sister when Kate stepped into the conference room. Lindsay gave her a friendly smile then turned back to her sister. "When you two are done, come and get me and we'll go for lunch."

On her way out of the room, Lindsay touched Kate's

shoulder. "I hear you and Jay found one of Hannah's potential fathers yesterday."

"Yes. We've sent a sample of his DNA to the lab."

"If he's the one, then you and Jay will be in stalemate."

"I know. I can't believe it." She let out a long breath then added, "He's got pretty good instincts for this work. I think we underestimated him."

"Well, hopefully Meg will help you get a jump on this next one." Lindsay patted her on the back in encouragement.

"Thanks."

Kate closed the door once Lindsay had gone, then turned to smile at her sister.

Meg was blonde like Lindsay, but not as tall and with softer features. In her well-cut gray suit, she looked the epitome of a downtown lawyer.

"Thanks so much for fitting me into your schedule." Kate shook Meg's hand and her fine-boned fingers felt so fragile, Kate was afraid she might hurt her.

"No problem. When Lindsay explained about the competition, I was fascinated. I'll be happy to help however I can."

Earlier Kate had e-mailed Meg the pertinent info on prospective dad number three. "Were you able to find out anything about Oliver Crane? I know he was admitted to the bar in Manhattan and I'm hoping he still works here."

Meg patted the sheet of paper in front of her. "You're in luck, Kate. He's a litigator at a small but extremely prestigious firm on Park Avenue. I have all his contact information here. E-mail, office address and phone numbers."

"Wonderful. Thank you so much." Kate couldn't stop a triumphant smile from spreading over her face. Oliver Crane had been even easier to find than James Morgan. Surely Jay wouldn't be one step ahead of her this time.

In order to keep her advantage, she had to schedule a meeting with Crane as soon as possible.

"There's something else I wanted to tell you, Kate, something I wasn't comfortable saying over the phone or in an e-mail."

Instantly alert, Kate leaned in closer.

"It turns out one of the partners at my firm, Susan Woodruff, used to work with Crane. According to Susan, Crane is ambitious and politically astute. And he doesn't mind trampling the little guy, if it helps him get ahead."

Kate made a face of distaste.

"These are just impressions, mind you. That's why I wanted to tell you in person. I wanted you to know the sort of person you would be dealing with."

"Thanks, Meg. I appreciate that." She was glad to have the information, though it was disappointing. Hopefully this man would *not* turn out to be Hannah's father.

But she'd rather rule out the possibility for certain than just *hope*.

"Can you tell me anything about his private life? Is he married?"

Meg nodded. "He and his wife have two children."

"So he may not be thrilled to discover he might have

a grown daughter he fathered with a woman he knew in college."

"Given his political aspirations, I'd say no, definitely not thrilled." Meg gave her a sympathetic smile. "I'd tread carefully with this one, if I were you."

CHAPTER NINE

AFTER THEIR MEETING, KATE and Meg met Lindsay for lunch at a vegetarian Thai restaurant. Most of their talk was about Lindsay and Nathan's wedding, which was scheduled for New Year's Eve.

"But that means we have to wait almost ten months," Meg wailed.

Lindsay wrapped some noodles deftly around her chopsticks. "Now you're sounding like Nathan. What's the rush? This way we have lots of time for planning."

"But you want a small, simple wedding."

Lindsay popped the noodles in her mouth, then gestured with her chopsticks. "Actually, I didn't want a wedding at all, remember? I was all for a quick visit to city hall."

Meg sighed, then turned to Kate. "This girl doesn't have a romantic bone in her body."

Kate grinned. "That's why she makes such a good investigator. But it doesn't explain the shoes."

They all looked under the table at Lindsay's coral Prada pumps. For some reason Lindsay could not walk past a good shoe sale. Ever.

"I like pretty shoes. I *am* a girl, you know."

"No doubt about that, sis." Meg turned her attention to Kate. "Lindsay told me that you just went through a big breakup. I'm sorry about that."

"Don't be sorry. It's for the best."

"You can say that again. You are way too good for that dirty, cheating, lousy bastard."

"Thanks, Lindsay. I'm beginning to think that I'd be better off having a family without a husband in the picture."

"Really? Are you thinking sperm bank?" Meg asked.

"You're not still considering that route, are you?" Lindsay shook her head. "Not a good idea. Kids are a lot of work, Kate. And money."

"I have an inheritance from my parents. I could afford to hire a nanny. And that's one of the reasons I wanted to work at Fox & Fisher, remember? No more shift work." She turned to Meg. "Shift work is hell on families."

"But Kate, a sperm bank? I know those guys are profiled, but there are intangible qualities to consider."

"Well, what are my options?" She thought about the bizarre conversation she'd had about this with Jay yesterday. For a moment she had thought Jay was going to volunteer his services.

Of course, he hadn't. They hardly knew one another.

If she told Meg and Lindsay that the two of them had even discussed this topic, they'd probably be shocked. On second thought, not too much shocked these women.

"I think you should start dating again," Lindsay said.

"No way. I am so through with that scene."

"Are you seriously giving up sex?" Lindsay looked as if the prospect was unimaginable.

"I wouldn't go that far. Just nothing too serious or complicated."

"What about that guy you're competing against?" Meg said. "I snuck a look at him on the way out. He's rather dashing, isn't he? And if he's a friend of Nathan's he must be a good guy."

"He's okay," Kate said, which was such an understatement she could hardly keep a straight face. "But he has a phobia about having kids."

"That's too bad," Meg said.

"Nathan, on the other hand, would have great sperm for babies." Kate turned to Lindsay. "What do you think of asking him if he'd be willing to make a donation to the cause?"

"What!" Noodles went flying as Lindsay choked on her last mouthful. "You're not serious, Kate?"

"Not at all." She smiled at Meg. "But it was fun to see your reaction."

BACK AT THE AGENCY, KATE retired to her office and closed the door. Jay was out for the moment and she had to make the most of her time alone.

She dialed the number Meg had given her for Oliver Crane and waited. A receptionist answered, her tone cool and impersonal.

"May I speak with Oliver Crane?" Kate asked.

"He's in a meeting. Who's calling, please?"

"Kate Cooper. I'm phoning on behalf of The Fox & Fisher Detective Agency, in regard to a personal matter."

"Oh." The receptionist sounded interested suddenly. "Can you be more specific?"

"I really need to speak to Mr. Crane in person."

"Well, then. Leave me your number and I'll have him call you when he has time."

The woman's tone suggested he might not have time for quite a while, but Kate left her number anyway. If she didn't hear back in a few hours, she would try sending an e-mail. But less than fifteen minutes later, her phone rang.

"Hello, Kate Cooper? Melissa passed on your message. What's this about?"

Immediately Kate decided that she needed to be face-to-face with this man before spilling the beans. If he decided to lie, it would be too easy over the phone. "I'd prefer to explain in person, at your convenience, of course. When you hear what it's about, I'm sure you'll understand."

"Is that necessary? I'm a very busy man."

And, by implication, a very *important* man. But Kate was counting on his curiosity being piqued. "It's a delicate matter, not something to discuss over the phone."

He sighed. "Fine. Meet me tomorrow morning at my gym." He named the place and the time, and Kate assured him she would be there.

"Thank you very much, Mr. Crane."

Kate disconnected the call, intrigued that he hadn't

wanted her to come to his office. She wondered if that meant he had more than one secret weighing on his conscience.

JAY KNEW HE COULDN'T SIT back and wait for the DNA results on James Morgan. He had to get busy and find the other two possible dads on Rebecca Trotter's list. Kate hadn't lost as much as an hour at work due to her cold, and he'd have to keep focused if he wanted to stay in the running.

It was hard not to worry about Eric, though. This morning he'd refused the toaster waffles Jay had set out for his breakfast. At least he'd downed a glass of orange juice before heading out the door with his usual grunt that seemed to pass for communication.

Had Eric been like this with his mother?

Jay wished he and Tracy had spent more time together the last few years. He should have bit his tongue where Tracy's boyfriend was concerned. Then maybe she'd have come to him when the louse left her, instead of turning to that bottle of pills.

He shouldn't have let that happen. But it had, and now Eric seemed like a stranger to him. He felt, instinctively, that he was doing the right thing in setting out rules and limits, but maybe he was pushing too hard.

All he'd managed to accomplish so far was to make his nephew resent him.

He needed to make a peace offering of some sort. Maybe a new cell phone—which Tracy had never been able to afford—was the answer. Most of the kids Eric's age seemed to own one, and that way he would be able to reach Eric at any time, which seemed pretty sensible.

Jay went out during his lunch hour to do some shopping. When he returned to the office around two, Kate was back at her desk. She was typing away on her keyboard at a rate that made him slightly anxious.

So far he'd accomplished exactly zero today as far as the case was concerned.

"Everything okay?" she asked.

"Sure. Fine." He opened the file on his desk purposefully, as if he, too, had important information to follow up on.

He stared at the blank page with Gary Gifford's name on the top. This guy had taken physical education at school. He'd also played on the football team for four years. Was it too much of a leap to assume he might have become a high school football coach after graduation?

Jay was initiating a simple Internet search when his cell phone rang. Kate's fingers paused over her keyboard as he said, "Savage here."

"I'm glad I reached you, Mr. Savage," a woman said, speaking in a serious tone. "I'm Police Officer Molly Bradford and I'm calling about your nephew, Eric. Were you aware that he didn't attend school today?"

Oh, hell. Jay felt as if someone had just given his head a spin. He struggled to focus. "Is he okay?"

"Eric is fine, but he was found hanging out around the Cathedral Parkway subway entrance during school hours."

"I guess he skipped classes." Again. "Is that a crime?"

"Have you heard about a program called TRACK?"

"No. What is it?"

"It's a partnership between the NYPD, the Department of Education and Administration for Children's Services. The idea is to keep school-age children in their classrooms where they belong. Basically, if a police officer finds school-age children loitering during class hours, they're brought in to a central location to be picked up by their parents or legal guardians."

She gave him a second to digest that, then asked, "Would you be able to pick up your nephew?"

"You bet I would." He wrote down the address she gave him, then promised he would be there as soon as possible.

Kate looked worried as he started to pack his papers into his briefcase. "Sorry. It was impossible for me not to hear that. Is Eric in trouble?"

"He skipped school." So much for his efforts last night. Dinner together, the chat about responsibilities. Obviously nothing had sunk in. "Have you heard of a program called TRACK?"

"Oh, yes. Is that where he is?"

"Yeah. An Officer Molly Bradford just called to say they had Eric."

"I've worked with Molly. She's a wonderful person. She really cares. And the TRACK program has been pretty successful at lowering crime rates among adolescents."

"Skipping school isn't a crime."

"No. But kids with too much spare time on their hands often find themselves in trouble."

Jay sighed. Why was he defending Eric? He knew the kid was headed down the wrong path. He just didn't have a clue what to do about it. He zipped his case closed then turned to leave.

"Jay?"

He waited to see what she wanted.

"I know Officer Bradford.... Would you like me to come with you?"

He instinctively shook his head no. But then he thought about it. He had nothing new to say to Eric. Maybe Kate, as a former police officer, would be able to reach him.

"I'm out of ideas on how to deal with the kid," he said wearily.

"Then let me come." She quickly closed down the computer. "Working with juvies was one of my specialties when I was with the police department."

KATE HADN'T BEEN ABLE to stop herself from volunteering to help once she'd seen the stricken look on Jay's face. She knew Jay had been worried Eric was making some poor choices. This pretty much proved it.

Once they'd hopped on board the northbound subway, Kate explained more about the TRACK program to Jay. "The idea is to keep kids in school and not on the street. The police bring them to a central holding location where they're screened with a metal-detecting wand, then made to sit quietly until their parents come to pick them up."

"Why don't they send them back to school?"

"The kids probably wish they would. They aren't

allowed to talk to one another. There's nothing to read, no cell phones or iPods. Lots of kids give out fake contact numbers, but when they realize the only way they're getting released is if a parent or guardian comes to pick them up, they eventually get cooperative."

Kate checked the sign on the subway wall. "This is our stop."

Jay followed her off the car, up several sets of stairs, then out to the street. Kate wrinkled her face against the cold wind and shoved her hands into her jacket pockets. "Over here," she said, directing him to an old brick building. They passed through a gate, then down a short flight of stairs.

"This is it," she said, leading him into a dimly lit auditorium.

"It's so quiet."

It was surprising, Kate agreed, given how many kids were packed into the space. A uniformed police officer sat at a desk near the entrance. Her black hair was braided tightly to her head and her dark chocolate eyes were serious and focused.

When she spotted Kate, however, her bright red lips broke out into a wide smile. "Hey, Cooper, how's it going?"

"I've quit the force," Kate told her. "I'm working for a private agency now."

Officer Bradford sighed. "And another one bites the dust." Her gaze shifted to Jay. "You two work together?"

"You could say that." He stepped forward to introduce himself. "I'm here for my nephew, Eric Savage."

"Ah. The quiet one. This is the first time we've picked him up, but when I phoned his school, I found out he's missed a lot of classes lately."

"Well, he's had a tough month. He lost his mother—my sister—at the end of February. Eric's had to move in with me and adjust to a whole new set of rules."

Officer Bradford's eyes widened with sympathy. "I'm sorry for your loss. Eric didn't say a thing. Just told me to call you rather than his mother."

"Yeah, well, he's not one for sharing."

"Mr. Savage, if you'd like some help dealing with your nephew, we could have a social service worker visit the home."

Kate watched him consider the offer. She knew he wanted the best for his nephew, but it wasn't easy turning to strangers for help.

"I might take you up on that, eventually," he finally said. "But I'd like to try one more time to work out a solution between the two of us."

"Well, here's a number to call in case you change your mind. And take my business card, too. If you're ever worried about Eric, you go right ahead and give me a call."

Jay shook her hand and thanked her.

"Now let me get Eric for you."

As Kate and Jay watched, Officer Bradford approached Eric and spoke to him quietly. Slowly Eric got to his feet, but as he walked toward his uncle, he avoided eye contact. He gave Kate one puzzled glance, then lowered his head again.

Finally Eric stood in front of Jay and neither one of them seemed to know what to say.

Stepping into the void, Kate put a hand on Eric's shoulder. "Hi, Eric. I'm Kate Cooper. I work at The Fox & Fisher Detective Agency with your uncle right now, but I used to work for the NYPD."

His gaze flew up. "You're a cop?"

"I used to be."

Eric whispered something under his breath. Kate wasn't sure, but she thought she'd heard him say, "Cool." It wasn't the response she'd expected from Jay's hard-nosed nephew.

"Let's get out of here so we can talk," Kate suggested.

"Good luck with that," Jay muttered, so only she could hear. Still, he followed behind them as Kate led the way to the street.

"Which way is home?" she asked Eric, and Jay kept quiet, leaving Eric to be the one to give directions.

"Sixty-ninth Street," Eric said. "We need to grab the subway."

"Why don't we walk," she suggested instead. It would take a long while to cover thirty blocks, but the exercise would do everyone good. And sometimes it was easier to talk when you didn't feel like everyone was staring at you.

There wasn't enough room on the sidewalk for three abreast, so Jay hung back and let Kate take the lead with his nephew. She was surprised when the young teenager started quizzing her about her former job on the police force.

"Why'd you decide to be a cop?"

"It's just something I always wanted. A lot of the people at the NYPD are the same—we grew up knowing what we wanted to do. Only in my case, I changed my mind."

She glanced back at Jay and saw him make a rueful face.

"Have you ever shot someone?"

"I've pulled my weapon, but never fired it on the job, thank God."

"Is it dangerous being a cop? Or do they just make it seem that way on TV?"

"Yes, it is dangerous. But we're trained to handle almost every situation you can imagine."

"Yeah? What kind of training?"

"Well, some of the training takes place in the class-room, reading and talking over various situations. But we run through simulations, too, where we basically act out dangerous scenarios and learn the correct proce-dures for handling them in real life."

"That sounds sweet. Why would you want to quit?"

"Working as an independent investigator is interest-ing, too. And you still get to help people, which is the part of the job that I like the most."

She waited a few moments, then asked, "Have you ever thought about what you'd like to do when you're finished school?"

"I'm not sure."

She wondered if that was true. "You need a high school degree for almost any kind of job or career."

"I know."

She glanced back at Jay, who was following the conversation with interest. He gave her a nod of encouragement.

"So why have you been skipping your classes?" she pressed gently. "Is there a problem with some of the kids, or maybe one of the teachers?"

"Mom never used to care if I went. She said school was boring and stupid."

"Do you find it boring?"

He lifted one shoulder, shifting his backpack at the same time. "Some of the classes are."

"When you get to high school, you'll have more say in choosing your courses. Maybe that will help."

"He has to get to high school first," Jay pointed out.

While correct, Kate wasn't sure Jay's comment was helpful. Eric's head drooped and he began walking slower. Perhaps he was just tired.

Eventually they ended up at a low-rise apartment building on Sixty-ninth Street. Eric leaned against the brick wall next to the entrance as Jay turned to Kate.

"Thanks for coming along."

"No problem." She frowned as she studied Eric. "Are you okay? Do you mind if I feel your forehead?"

When he shrugged, she leaned forward and slipped her hand under his blond curls. His skin seemed very warm to her but was it just from the long walk? "How do you feel?"

Eric said nothing, but Jay stepped forward for a closer look at his nephew.

"He didn't eat much for dinner or breakfast. I think

you're right, Kate. Maybe he caught that bug that's going around."

"My throat's kind of sore. A lot of kids at school are sick," Eric allowed.

"How would you know?" Jay asked. "You haven't been there much lately."

Eric flushed and Jay seemed to regret his sarcastic comment. "That's okay, Eric. We'll talk about this later. Right now I think you need some sleep."

"And maybe some chicken soup," Kate added. "That's what I always feel like when I'm under the weather."

"I have some cans in the cupboard," Jay said. "We'll see what we can find. Thanks again, Kate." He touched her arm. "Are you headed home? Would you like me to call you a cab?"

"It's not far. I'll walk." She started down the sidewalk, then turned back. "Take care of yourself, Eric. It was nice to meet you."

The teenager gave her a tepid wave before following his uncle in the main door.

Kate stood in place a moment, uneasy for some reason at leaving the two behind. There was so much tension between them. She wished she could understand why. Eric had certainly been polite enough with *her*. But he didn't have much to say to his uncle.

Finally the cold forced her to start walking again. When she passed by a market, she decided to stop in for some groceries and found herself selecting all the ingredients she needed for homemade chicken soup.

As she waited at the till, she noticed a young mother

in the lineup beside her. The healthy, plump woman had what looked to be a four-month-old in a chest carrier. The baby was awake and curious, trying to touch the gold studs in the mother's ears.

"What an adorable baby," Kate couldn't help commenting. The little one was in a purple snowsuit with a green hat. "Boy or girl?"

"Girl." The young mother flashed her a tired smile, then set a tin of baby formula and a package of diapers on the conveyer belt. The baby reached once more for the earrings. "Stop that, Emma darling," the mother said, taking her baby's fingers and kissing them.

"That will be thirty-seven fifty, please."

"Sorry?" Suddenly Kate realized the clerk was speaking to her. She paid for her groceries, then left the store, a familiar yearning spreading through her and pressing against her rib cage.

I want a baby.

She stepped outside and let the March wind snap her quickly back to reality. She wasn't married and had no prospects of getting pregnant. She would do better to concentrate on her career right now.

At home, after dinner, she should spend some time on the Internet. But home was such a quiet place these days. And she couldn't forget the look she had seen in Eric's eyes. The sadness that she suspected lay deeper in his soul than the anger and sullenness he displayed to his uncle.

She headed back toward Jay's apartment and rang the bell. "Hi, it's Kate. If I'm not imposing, I thought I would make you and Eric some soup for dinner."

CHAPTER TEN

IN HER YEARS WITH THE NYPD, Kate had learned how to read a New York City apartment pretty accurately. Jay's held no surprises. Good-quality leather furniture, functional lamps and a large, flat-screen TV marked him as a single, well-salaried male. The framed photographs on the wall—sky shots which could only have been taken from a cockpit—identified him as a pilot.

Eric was already asleep on the sofa, so she trod quietly to take a closer look at the three pictures. "These are amazing."

One photo captured a floor of cotton-ball clouds in a broad expanse of cornflower-blue sky. Another showed the sun setting on the Sierra Madre range reflecting bands of earthy pinks and orange and violet. And the final one, perhaps the most impressive, was an electrical storm at night, taken from a vantage point that few people ever experience.

"That lightning looks awfully close. Were you terrified?"

"Electrical storms are always a danger. But we're

trained to navigate our way through storm lines. If you can't find a soft spot on the radar, then you have to reroute."

She continued down the hall to the kitchen, where Jay had already set out her groceries. Music was playing softly from an iPod dock on the counter and a bottle of sparkling water was opened next to a couple of glasses.

Jay handed her one of the glasses. "This is very nice of you, Kate."

"Not so nice. My evenings are pretty free these days." As she sipped the water, she studied the layout of the cabinets, then took a guess and opened one. Inside she found the large pot she'd been looking for. She filled it two-thirds with water, then added the chicken pieces she'd bought at the store.

"You're boiling the chicken?"

"I'm making stock."

"What can I do?"

She handed him an onion, one of the carrots and a stalk of celery. "Chop these coarsely and add them to the pot."

"So what's your plan?" Jay asked as he set to work.

"You mean for finding Hannah's father?"

"No. For filling those free evenings of yours."

She turned up the heat on the stove. "My short-term plan is to get a kitten."

"And long-term?"

"I already told you what I want," she said softly.

"Children."

"Yes."

Jay added the chopped vegetables to the pot. "A woman like you should be able to have it all. A husband

and kids *and* a cat. Hell, you could probably even go for a dog if you were greedy."

He passed her a wooden spoon, and she gave the pot a stir. "You make it sound so easy."

"I just think you should hold out for the whole package. If that's what you want."

She turned the burner to simmer, then covered the pot. Already a delicious aroma was filling the kitchen. "I wonder if my hurry to start a family clouded my judgment where Conner was concerned. And I'm worried the same thing could happen again."

"You don't strike me as the sort of person to make the same mistake twice."

"So I make a different mistake next time." She shrugged. "Wouldn't I be better off having a child and taking the pressure off my biological clock? Then if I meet the right guy, great. The whole package is still possible."

"That doesn't strike you as a little backward? Having the baby first, and finding the husband later?"

"Not really. No." She thought of the cute baby at the grocery store and sighed. "We need to chop more vegetables. These are for the soup, not the broth, so they need to be much finer."

She showed Jay what she meant and they worked together in comfortable silence for a while. Only, it wasn't that comfortable. She was very aware of Jay's presence, of his wide shoulders, his strong, capable hands.

He moved around the kitchen with ease, yet never lost that aura of masculine authority that seemed to be bred into his bones. She suspected Eric looked up to his uncle far more than Jay realized. The sullen behavior was just a mask. But what had put it there was a mystery to her.

When it came time to strain the broth, Jay lifted the large pot while she held a colander over a second pot. Once the bones had been discarded, she added the freshly chopped veggies and some herbs.

"What about you?" she asked as she wiped down the counters. "Now that you're not flying around the world anymore, how are you going to meet women?"

"Dating is the last thing on my mind right now." His gaze drifted toward the living room.

She didn't need to wonder what was worrying him.

"It sounds like his mother didn't place much importance on education."

"Tracy wasn't mean or abusive. She just didn't put much effort into raising Eric. Given the example our mother set for her, I guess I can't blame her."

"What was Tracy like?"

"She was sweet and pretty. But all she cared about was having a good time. She also seemed to be a magnet for jerks. So maybe it was a good thing that none of her romances lasted long."

"What about Eric's father?"

"Oh, he took off as soon as he found out Tracy was pregnant. Never been heard from since."

"Have you ever tried to find him? For the support payments if nothing else?"

"Nah. No point with a guy like that."

Kate nodded. She had seen too many of that type in her years as a cop. "Well, that's tough on Eric."

"He hasn't had an easy go of it," Jay agreed. "Living with Tracy couldn't have been fun. One minute she was ecstatically happy, the next despondent. It was her latest breakup that triggered the overdose that killed her."

Kate winced. What a brutal summary of a tragic death. "I'm sorry."

"The guy at the heart of it all didn't even show up to her memorial service." He gave her a halfhearted smile. "No wonder Eric's a mess, huh? I should have made more of an effort with him."

"Did you see him very often?"

"When he was younger. Once Tracy no longer needed a babysitter, though, she started to avoid me. I guess she was tired of the lectures about her drinking and her boyfriends and I just couldn't stop myself from giving them." He rubbed the back of his neck, his expression so weary and full of guilt, it made her heart ache.

Eric's life had been tough. But as far as she could see, Jay's had been just as difficult. "Hopefully Eric will learn from his mother's mistakes and start going to his classes."

"If he does, it'll probably be thanks to you. You were really communicating with him today. There's definitely something special about you, Kate Cooper."

They were standing several feet apart, yet Kate could feel the warmth in his gaze as he looked at her. There was gratitude in his expression, but something else, too.

She felt connected to him in a way she couldn't explain. And attracted in a way she didn't want to acknowledge. Neither one of them was looking for a relationship right now. Was it possible that made them perfect for each other?

She dried her hands, then said briskly, "In fifteen minutes, add the egg noodles to the broth. When they're cooked, the soup will be ready to serve."

As she headed toward the door, he asked, "Aren't you going to stay and eat with us?"

She shook her head. "The soup is for Eric. I hope he feels better soon."

And then she left, because she was afraid of what might happen if she stayed any longer.

WHEN ERIC WOKE UP, Jay filled a bowl with chicken soup, then brought it to the living room and set it on the coffee table.

"Do you feel like eating anything?"

"I'll give it a try." Eric leaned over the table, then took a spoonful. "Not bad."

"Kate made it for you."

"Yeah?" Eric nodded. "She's nice."

Jay couldn't agree more, which left him feeling pretty conflicted about the competition between them. But what could he do? He *needed* this job.

He went back to the kitchen to grab the sandwich he'd made for himself, then returned to the living room to eat it.

When they were both finished with dinner, he braced himself to say what needed to be said.

"You've got to start going to school, Eric. Every day. No skipping."

Eric gave him an indolent stare. "Yeah?"

"This is nonnegotiable."

"What'll you do if I don't do it? Call that number for social services? Maybe put me into foster care?"

Jay felt sucker punched. "Why would you say something like that?"

"I'm cramping your style, right? First you had to rearrange your apartment to make room for me. Then you had to quit flying. You'd probably be dating that hot redhead right now if I wasn't around."

"Boy, have you got things wrong."

Eric set his mouth mutinously.

"First off, I wouldn't be dating Kate Cooper. She's looking for something I can't give her. And secondly, of course, I made room for you in my home. You're family."

"Whatever that means."

Jay clenched his jaw, holding back an angry response. He couldn't let this disintegrate into a shouting match between the two of them.

He took a deep breath. "It means you're stuck with me. And you're stuck having to go to school. Got it?"

Eric glared at him.

Damn it, the kid had sounded almost normal when he'd been talking to Kate. Fifteen minutes with him, and Eric was back to being a rebellious, out-of-control teenager.

Jay took the dirty dishes to the kitchen and wished he had even a clue about what to do next.

THE NEXT MORNING Eric's fever was gone, so Jay insisted he get up and get ready for school. He'd already decided he wasn't going to start work until he was certain that Eric was on school property.

His nephew was sullen and uncommunicative as usual, even when Jay handed him the new cell phone.

"What's this for?"

"It's yours. I signed up for the basic plan. No voice mail, but you have unlimited local calls and text messages."

Eric turned the phone over in his hand, as if he were trying to find something wrong with it.

"I've programmed my numbers in there," Jay said. "Home, cell phone and office."

"Oh, I get it. This is so you can keep better tabs on me."

Hell. There was no winning with this kid. Jay grabbed his briefcase and his keys. "Come on, let's get going. You don't want to be late."

"I've got a few minutes. You go ahead."

"I don't think so." Jay held the door open and waited as Eric slipped into his running shoes.

"What are you going to do?" Eric asked as he shuffled out into the hall. "Hold my hand and walk me into my classroom?"

"If I have to."

AS SOON AS HE STEPPED outdoors, Jay's foot sank through several inches of fresh snow.

The storm must have passed through last night and now the city looked as clean as a miracle. But the dirty sludge was still underfoot, frozen into dangerous patches of ice. "Watch your step," he warned Eric as he felt his own feet sliding beneath him.

"It'll be a mess at the airport," Jay commented, mostly to himself. He thought about things he didn't miss in his former career: deicing, slippery runways, muddled schedules and grumpy passengers.

The subway ride with Eric wasn't pleasant. They basically ignored one another, then moving in concert, disembarked at the Cathedral Parkway station.

Without a word, Eric started walking toward his school and Jay hurried to catch up, several feet stretched between them, until they reached the boundary of school property.

Then Jay stopped. "Look, I know that as soon as I turn my back, you can leave if you want to."

"No kidding."

"I'm asking you not to. Please, Eric. Go to school. Do it for yourself. For your future."

Eric dropped his gaze. Jay had no idea if his words had reached him, if anything he had to say mattered to the boy anymore. They stood there awhile, neither one saying a word. Then Eric turned and began to trudge toward the school.

Jay watched until Eric had disappeared inside, then checked his watch. He was running so late, he decided he would take a taxi to the office. Holding up his arm, he signaled to a yellow cab he could see just down the block.

As KATE RUSHED through the new fallen snow toward the subway station, she battled an uneasy feeling of guilt. There was nothing underhanded about her going to the gym to meet Oliver Crane without telling Jay.

They weren't supposed to be working as a team. She was doing nothing wrong.

Yet after yesterday, seeing him in his home and with his nephew, she couldn't help wondering if he needed this job more than she did. She hurried down the stairs and spotted a train at the platform. She dashed past the doors just before they slid shut and grabbed for a pole as the car lurched forward.

But this was always supposed to be her job, she reminded herself, steeling her resolve to win. Lindsay had tried to woo her to the agency so many times. It really did suck that when she was finally ready to say yes, Nathan had to have promised the same job to one of his friends.

She supposed she was feeling conflicted, because she was used to working as part of a team—not as adversaries. And also, perhaps, she had allowed herself to develop too much of a friendship with Jay.

He was her competition. She should be treating him like the enemy.

Keeping people at arm's length had never been her way. Still, she resolved to talk to him later. To remind him that she wanted this job and she intended to get it. Just because she'd made his nephew a batch of chicken soup last night, he shouldn't expect her to go easy on him.

The train screeched to a stop and she scrambled out with a score of other passengers. Like a river, the mass of them flowed along the platform, then up the stairs before spilling out to the gray, snowy city sidewalks.

Kate waded through the muck toward a big stone building across from Central Park. The Athletic Club was an institution in the city, and it was a measure of Oliver Crane's success that he had managed to obtain a membership.

Once inside, she made her way to the lounge just past the reception area, as she'd been instructed, taking the liberty of ordering two fresh juice cocktails before settling at a small table.

Oliver Crane kept her waiting twenty minutes, which didn't surprise her. Consideration for other people didn't strike her as one of his strong suits. When he finally arrived, she had no difficulty picking him out from the crowd. Though his hair was thinner and touched with gray, his ears still stuck out the way they had in his university yearbook.

She stood to shake his hand, then gave him one of Lindsay's business cards. He glanced down at it and frowned.

"I thought you said your name was Kate Cooper."

"It is. I wrote my name and number on the back of the card. I'm representing The Fox & Fisher Detective Agency, which is why I wanted you to have their name and number, as well."

"So what is this matter you're so urgent to discuss in private?"

She waved him to the empty chair and offered him the juice cocktail, which he accepted grudgingly. So far, she was not impressed with this man. He was rude, self-important and, she suspected, chronically grouchy. Had he always been that way, she wondered, or had a career as a Wall Street lawyer corrupted him?

There must have been something fun or charming about him at one time to attract Rebecca Wagner.

"Our agency has been retained to find the biological father of Hannah Young. Her mother identified you as a possibility. You would have known her as Rebecca Wagner."

His eyes flashed wide at the mention of that name. A moment later, though, his expression was cool and disinterested. "I don't remember anyone by that name."

"Did you go to New England College in 1984?"

"Yes, but so did a lot of guys."

"Well, Rebecca only slept with three of them."

"And you think I was one of that select group?" he asked, in a tone of prissy superiority. "I'm afraid I must disagree."

Kate hadn't expected an outright lie from the man, but she had come prepared. She dug the photocopied pages from the yearbook out of her carry case and showed him Rebecca's photograph. "Does this refresh your memory?"

He studied the picture carefully, then shook his head. "Afraid not."

Now Kate was getting angry. "Hannah isn't looking for money, or support of any kind. She just wants to find out about her health history before she starts a family of her own."

For a moment she thought Oliver Crane would capitulate. Then his lips thinned and he shook his head. He set aside the fruit juice and placed her card on the table.

"You've come to the wrong man. You'll have to keep looking."

She had *not* found the wrong man, but she realized she had nothing to gain by pushing any further today. Instead, she picked up her card and slipped it into his jacket pocket as she rose from her seat. He didn't notice, nor did he wait to help her with her coat or to walk with her to the street. He just took off as if he never wanted to see her again, which she was certain was the case.

Kate hoped that later—maybe a few hours, maybe a few days—he would find that business card, and his conscience would give him a good hard nudge.

She hoped. But she didn't count on it.

CHAPTER ELEVEN

WHEN KATE ARRIVED back at the office, Nadine got up from behind her desk to greet her. "The DNA results haven't arrived yet," she said. "And Jay's in the office. I don't think he's in a very good mood."

Their well-dressed receptionist was wearing sleek brown boots today, with knee-length wool trousers, a hip, metallic belt and a red sweater. Somehow all these disparate elements came together to make perfect fashion sense on Nadine.

Kate helped herself to coffee. "Thanks for the update."

Nadine looked at her expectantly. "Well? Did you get another DNA sample?" she asked in a hushed voice.

"Afraid not." Oliver Crane was beginning to look like a lost cause. Her only hope now was to find Gary Gifford. As long as they were able to test the DNA of two of the three men, they would still be able to tell Hannah and her husband which one was her father.

The door to the office she shared with Jay was open. He was just wrapping up a phone call when she entered, and she found herself smiling at him, heart skipping like a teenager's when he smiled back.

"Okay. I'll see you shortly." He closed his phone. "Hi, Kate. I was wondering when you would show up."

Guilt nudged at her again, and she resolved to set things straight, right here and now.

"I was following up a lead. Didn't go as well as I hoped."

"I'd like to say I was sorry, but I can't really do that. Look, Kate—"

"Wait a minute. There's something I need to say to you. About yesterday. Coming with you to get your nephew, then making that soup… You didn't ask me to do any of that, I just sort of pushed my way in."

"Pushed? You were helping. And I really appreciated it."

"Thanks. I'm glad you think that way. But I need to make sure you understand that I still want the job at Fox & Fisher. I'm still determined to find Hannah's father and solve the case before you do."

"You didn't need to explain. I wouldn't have expected anything else."

She was relieved to hear him say that. And yet, a tiny part of her felt disappointed, too. "Good. I'm glad we're clear on that."

"Me, too. Because I'm determined to win this competition, as well." He grabbed a sheaf of paper from his desk and shoved it into his briefcase. "See you later, Kate. I've got a lead of my own."

THE CAB ROUNDED a corner and Bishop High School came into view. "This is it," Jay told the driver. "You can stop at the corner."

One of the copilots he flew with—correction, *had* flown with—had a brother, Bob St. Clair, who taught physical education and coached at the high school level. Jay realized he was clutching at straws, but he was hoping that Bob might be able to tell him if Gary Gifford was teaching in the public school system, too.

There were probably smarter ways of trying to track a teacher. Undoubtedly Kate knew all the right databases and Internet searches to use. But he didn't and he had his fingers crossed that Bob St. James would steer him in the right direction.

He paid his fare, then stepped onto a newly shoveled sidewalk. It was ten in the morning and the school grounds were quiet. Undoubtedly all the students were inside attending classes. Jay's mood lightened as he followed the paved path to the front doors of the three-story brick building.

When he was a kid, school had been a refuge for him, and he'd been mostly happy there. Because his mother had moved them frequently, he'd often had to deal with being the "new kid" and he'd learned how to make friends quickly. Being athletic hadn't hurt. Joining teams was a great way to belong, which was why he'd been so keen for Eric to play basketball.

Jay reported at the school reception and was told that he could find Coach Bob at the gym.

This was familiar territory to Jay. The hardwood

floors and basketball hoops, the big round clocks and the pennants proudly displayed on the wall. And the smell.

A group of kids, both girls and guys, were playing volleyball under the supervision of a woman in her thirties, with dark hair, cut athletically short.

"Looking for someone?" she called out to him.

"Bob St. Clair?"

"That's his office." She pointed, then returned her attention to her students.

The coach's office was a small, disorganized place, filled with files and papers, trophies and other sporting memorabilia. Coach Bob was about ten years older than Jay, with a round face and friendly eyes.

"Nice to meet you, Jay." He stood up to shake hands. "My brother told me all about you. That time you didn't know if the landing gear had come down...that must have been something, huh?"

Jay had forgotten that he and Wayne had been together on that flight. The incident fell under the category of near-disasters he'd rather forget, but Coach Bob wasn't easily dissuaded. "What did it feel like when the landing gear didn't lock? Did you ever think you wouldn't make it?"

"A pilot has no business thinking that way. When something goes wrong, you concentrate on your job. Flying the plane remains number one. Then trouble-shooting the problem. If you have any spare time above that, you spend it reassuring the crew and the passengers and keeping everyone calm and focused."

"Wayne said he couldn't believe how cool you were. He said he was sweating bullets."

"He was young. Experience counts for a lot in a situation like that."

"Though you don't want too many of those experiences, do you?"

"That's for sure."

"Well." Ice-breaking chitchat over, the coach splayed his hands on his desk. "How can I help you? According to my brother's e-mail, you're trying to find a football coach by the name of Gary Gifford."

"That's the right name, but he may not be coaching. All I know for sure is that he played football for the Blue Devils from 1984 to 1988 when he graduated from New England College with a degree in physical education."

"Well, Gary's a coach all right. Or he was. Last place I traced him was Brooklyn Heights High School, two years ago."

"Two years ago? Where did he go after that?"

"No one knows." Coach Bob shrugged. "But if you want details, I'd talk to Travis Johnson. He's Gary's replacement."

"Well, thanks for the tip. I appreciate that."

"No problem. And when this investigation—or whatever it is you're doing—is over, you get back to flying planes. You hear?"

Yeah, right. I wish. Jay thanked Coach St. Clair again for his time and left.

KATE DIDN'T KNOW if Jay WAS bluffing, or if he really did have a genuine lead. Not that it mattered. She'd gone as far as she could with Oliver Crane. That left only one man to find: Gary Gifford.

She pulled out her spreadsheet to review everything she knew about him. This was the guy who had been on the college football team, the guy who had graduated with a degree specializing in physical education. It made sense that he would end up with a job teaching in a school somewhere. But that somewhere could be anywhere.

Kate searched databases diligently for several hours without finding Gary's name in any of the current listings. She started with Manhattan, then all the boroughs, slowly expanding her search through most of the state. Finally she had to face the fact that he might not be teaching in the public school system. Perhaps he'd landed a coaching job with one of the college football teams. Or found a job in another part of the country.

She abandoned her database searches and started entering random combinations with Gary's name into Google. In just ten minutes she located an article written two years ago in the *Brooklyn Newspaper*. Gary Gifford was profiled in a story about teachers who made a difference. According to the article, he was a teacher and coach at Brooklyn Heights High School.

Kate printed off the article, then searched for the school's phone number. When she asked for Gary Gifford, however, the school receptionist replied that he had retired a few years ago.

"He wasn't that old, was he?"

"He took early retirement."

The receptionist sounded a little impatient. Almost

as if she'd already been asked this same question once today. Could it be? No, surely not, Kate told herself. Jay simply couldn't be one step ahead of her this time.

"I'm afraid I can't tell you much more than that," the receptionist concluded.

Surely someone at the school had to know more. "Who replaced him?"

"Travis Johnson," was the weary reply.

"May I speak to him, please?" She waited while the call was transferred, then ended up having to leave a message. It was three o'clock, Kate noted. Probably Travis Johnson was in class. Rather than wait for him to check his messages and call her back, she decided to take a cab out to the school and try to catch him before he went home for the day.

Grabbing her leather bag, she left the office, stopping in the reception area for her coat.

"Now where?" Nadine asked, her eyes bright.

"Brooklyn Heights High School." She fastened the belt on her jacket. Had she imagined the flash of amusement in Nadine's eyes? "If Jay asks, you won't say anything?"

"Of course not," Nadine assured her.

Kate paused to give the receptionist a probing look. Nadine smiled, but remained silent.

Kate couldn't resist. She had to ask. "Do you know where Jay is this afternoon?"

Nadine kept smiling.

"I was afraid of that. Damn it!" Kate ran down the stairs and along the street, praying for a cab to appear quickly.

ABOUT TWENTY TEENAGE boys in school uniforms were running around the schoolyard when Kate's cab pulled up in front of Brooklyn Heights High School. The coach, a short man with immense shoulders, was standing on the edge of the field, holding a clipboard and talking to Jay.

He really had beaten her here. How the hell did he keep doing that?

Kate paid her fare, then stepped out to the street. Jay was about thirty yards away, but she could see his face quite clearly. He looked amused, darn him. Then he continued speaking, in an animated fashion, to the coach.

As she picked her way carefully through the snow and slush in her high-heel boots, she wondered how the kids managed to run in these conditions. As she drew closer, she saw that snow had been removed from an oval track that ran the circumference of the school property. Most of the kids threw her curious glances, but the coach had his back to her and didn't even notice her until she had joined them.

"Sorry I'm late, Jay," she said. "Nadine forgot to give me the message."

Jay's smile broadened, and he looked like he was going to laugh. At least he wasn't upset that she'd found him here and was barging into yet another one of his prearranged meetings.

It was hard not to appreciate how handsome he looked in his sheepskin jacket and dark jeans. He was wearing his aviator sunglasses again, and with his killer smile, he was good-looking enough to draw glances from a group of girls who were standing, shivering, near the side entrance of the school, probably waiting for the boys to finish practice.

Jay played along with her charade. "Let me bring you up to speed. Travis, this is Kate Cooper. She's working on this case, too. Kate, Travis Johnson. Travis was just explaining that Gary took early retirement a few years ago."

She hadn't noticed, until then, the way the coach was looking at her—as if she were a piece of candy on a tray.

"Nice to meet you, Kate. Do you live in Brooklyn?"

She saw him check out her hands, undoubtedly noting the lack of rings. "No. Manhattan. Upper West Side." She tucked her hands into the deep pockets of her coat and gave him a cautious smile in return. Friendly, but not too much so. "Gary was in his mid-forties. Why did he take early retirement? Was there a problem?"

Travis Johnson seemed affronted by the suggestion. "You mean some sort of scandal? Not at all. Gary was a great guy and a gifted teacher. I worked with him for a few weeks before he left. I gathered he was leaving for health issues. But he didn't provide details."

"Did he keep in touch after he left?"

"Not with me."

"I worked my way through the staff room earlier," Jay added for her benefit. "Seems Gary hasn't kept in touch with anyone here."

It was generous of him to share his information, though it was unfortunate this school seemed to be a dead end.

She glanced at the coach again. He was still eyeing

her with interest. If she wasn't currently off men, she might have given him an encouraging smile. He was nice-looking, athletic and, obviously being a coach and a teacher, he must like kids.

She felt zero romantic interest, though.

"Is there anything else you can tell us about Gary?" Kate asked, hoping for a hint of where to look next. "Do you know if he had any family or any particular hobbies or interests?"

"He wasn't married. I heard rumors from the kids that he was in love with one of the teachers here. But you know how kids talk. As for other interests, far as I know, all he really cared about was sports. Particularly football, of course."

Coach Johnson blew a whistle, then called out for the guys on the field to hit the showers. As the young guys streamed off the field into the school, the coach trailed behind with her and Jay.

"I'm sorry I couldn't be more helpful." The coach was looking at Kate as he said this. "Maybe you could leave your number, though. In case I find something else."

"I've already left my number on your answering machine," Kate said. "Please do contact us if you or any of your fellow teachers remember anything about Gary."

Travis glanced quickly from Kate to Jay. "You two…you just work together, right?"

"So far," Jay said, before Kate had a chance to reply. He winked at Travis, who reacted with confusion, then a nervous chuckle.

"Thanks again for your time," Kate said, mildly annoyed at Jay. As they left the school grounds together, she decided to put him in his place. "Why did you say *so far,* as if there might be a relationship between us in the future?"

"I could see the guy was interested in you. I was just trying to give you an easy out."

"But what if I wanted him to be interested?"

"Just last night you said you were done with dating. Did meeting Coach Johnson inspire you to change your mind?"

The idea was ludicrous, leaving Kate to wonder why she felt so upset. Was it because she could take care of herself and Jay shouldn't have butted in? Or was it because his interest in claiming her affections had only been faked?

ALTHOUGH IT WAS ALREADY five o'clock, Kate opted to return to the office and Jay decided to do the same.

During the cab ride back to Manhattan, Kate quizzed Jay on how he had traced Gary Gifford to Brooklyn Heights High School. Again, he impressed her with his resourcefulness. Even though he didn't have her training and experience, somehow his instincts always seemed to lead him to the right place.

In the office, she was surprised to see Nadine still seated at her desk.

"I'm so glad you came back." Nadine broke into a relieved smile. "I was worried you'd go straight home after your meeting at the school."

"You knew Jay was going to be there when I told you where I was headed, didn't you?"

Nadine put up her hands in an apologetic gesture. "I'm sorry. I hate being in the middle, but I have to be impartial. Really, I wish *both* of you could win."

"At this point I don't think either of us is going to solve this case." Kate flopped onto the reception area sofa and grabbed a handful of the jelly beans meant for waiting clients.

Though they'd warned Hannah that finding her father could take weeks, Kate hadn't really expected the job to be this tough.

Jay sat next to her. He, too, appeared tired. "We came so close…"

"Maybe you're closer than you think." Nadine held up a thick envelope. "Look what the courier dropped off one hour ago. The DNA test results for James Morgan."

CHAPTER TWELVE

"Okay," Nadine asked, holding the envelope from BioFinds Lab in her hands. "Who's going to open this?"

Kate glanced at Jay. He was looking at her. He raised an eyebrow and shrugged, and she guessed that, like her, he didn't know what to hope for.

A positive result would be best for Hannah. It wouldn't matter that Oliver Crane had refused to provide a DNA sample or that the trail had gone cold on Gary Gifford. She would be free to get pregnant without worries and James would suddenly have a daughter and a grandchild.

But then there would be no clear winner in the competition. Lindsay and Nathan would be no further ahead in deciding which of them should get the job.

"I feel like we're presenting at the Oscars," Jay said. "You open the envelope, and I'll read the results."

"I can't believe how nervous I feel." Kate took the envelope from Nadine, hesitated, then tore it open. Inside was the report. She handed it to Jay.

"And the winner is…" He paused to read silently for a moment, then his shoulders sank.

"There is no winner," Jay confirmed. "Because James Morgan is *not* the father."

"That's bad, isn't it? Or is it good?" Nadine looked from Kate to Jay, trying to judge their reactions. "At least this way one of you still has a chance of winning."

It was so like Nadine to try and put a positive spin on the results. "That's true," Kate said. "But I'm not looking forward to telling James Morgan the news. He and his wife were so excited about this. I feel like I raised their hopes for nothing."

"I'll make the call," Nadine said.

"That's sweet of you to offer. But I took his DNA sample. I feel like I should be the one to phone with the results."

"Are you sure?" Jay asked quietly. "I was there, too. It could just as easily be me."

"We could make it a conference call," Nadine suggested. "That way you could both be on the line when you tell him."

Kate looked at Jay. He nodded.

"That's a great idea, Nadine," she said. "Jay can use the phone in our office and I'll grab the one in the conference room."

"Okay." Nadine started to arrange the call, then paused. "Oh, one more thing I should mention now before I forget."

Kate and Jay waited for her to continue.

"Lindsay and Nathan wanted me to tell you both that they've arranged a progress report with Hannah Young and her husband for tomorrow morning at nine."

JAMES MORGAN HANDLED the disappointing news much better than Kate had expected.

"Ah, well, I guess it wasn't meant to be," he said sanguinely. "Thanks for letting me know. And good luck finding your client's father. I hope he turns out to be a worthy man."

"We really appreciate your cooperation," Jay said.

"And good luck to you, too, Jimmy." Kate disconnected the call and sat for a moment, stumped.

She'd expected him to be so crushed. Maybe she'd just projected her own desperate desire to have children onto Jimmy and his wife. They'd obviously been a happy and content couple before she and Jay had arrived with their outrageous request. And now they still would be.

Jay appeared at the open door to the conference room. "That went well."

"Surprisingly well."

He glanced at his watch. "Nadine just left. She wants us to lock up. Are you ready to go?"

Kate thought about the meeting tomorrow morning with the client. It would be easier to prepare a report here at the office than at home. "No. I think I'll stay a while longer. You go ahead. I'll make sure everything is locked up safely for the night."

But Jay didn't leave. He stepped into the room and closed the door. "I don't know about you, but I'm kind of at a standstill with the case right now."

She hesitated, then sighed. "Me, too. What a disappointment that the trail went cold at Brooklyn Heights High School."

Disappointing, but not unusual. Most cases had their moments of progress and inevitable setbacks. She was far from ready to give up. But Jay didn't have the same experience to draw from. Maybe he was becoming discouraged.

"When I saw you get out of the cab at the high school today, I didn't know whether to laugh or cry."

"I felt much the same way when I saw you."

They exchanged reluctantly amused glances.

"You're pretty good at this stuff," she said. "But I'm still going to beat you."

"Love your confidence, woman."

"It's well founded," she assured him. "I hope you have a plan for what you'll do if you don't get this job."

"Losing isn't an option as far as I'm concerned. Maybe you should come up with a good alternative."

She shook her head.

"You could go back to the police department," Jay suggested.

"If you'd read my letter of resignation, you wouldn't say that."

Jay grinned. "Burned a few bridges, did you?"

"I couldn't help myself. It was an emotional time and I felt like everyone in the precinct knew about Conner's affair except me."

"Ugly gossip travels fast," he agreed. "But just because no one said anything to you, you shouldn't assume they weren't on your side. Sometimes people are afraid to interfere."

"Maybe so. But even if Conner hadn't been such a

cheating skunk, I was still ready for a change. I learned a lot working for the NYPD, but I'm not prepared to make the sacrifices that are necessary for a long-term career."

"Not conducive to a good family life, huh?"

"Especially if you're a single parent."

He tilted his head to one side. "You're still considering going that route?"

She nodded.

"So why weren't you more encouraging when Travis Johnson hit on you today?"

"He hit on me?"

"Right. I'm not buying that innocent act. You know very well he was interested. And you didn't give him the least amount of encouragement. But maybe you're still hung up on your ex-fiancé...."

"Absolutely not."

"Then why not give Travis a chance? I'm just a guy, what do I know, but he seemed decently attractive. And he's healthy and athletic. As a teacher and coach he'd be bound to make a great father."

All points that she'd noticed on her own. Yet, it hadn't mattered. "Maybe he's not my type."

"And you can know that after a fifteen-minute conversation?"

It wasn't logical, she knew, but the answer was yes. She had known. Just as she'd known when she'd met Jay, that if circumstances were different...

She swallowed. "Maybe I should call him. Suggest going out for a drink. Is that what you want?"

Jay's expression darkened. "Hell, no. When he was hitting on you, I wanted to throttle the guy."

Jay had no reason to feel territorial about her, and yet she felt a crazy thrill that he did. "You seemed amused."

"Look behind the smile next time. I was clenching my teeth so hard, I'm surprised they didn't crack."

She went to the credenza. Her movements felt stiff and self-conscious as she poured herself a glass of water. Behind her, she heard his chair squeak as he stood up. When he spoke again, he was right behind her.

"I can't explain why I felt that way. I know I have no right."

She sipped the cool water. He was standing at least two feet away, but she felt the warmth from his body all around her.

"We hardly know each other." She licked her lips nervously. "But yesterday I was thinking that might be a good thing."

"Oh? This sounds fascinating. Please explain."

She turned to face him. "Neither one of us is interested in a relationship right now. But—we still have needs."

Jay's eyes narrowed. She swallowed, experiencing his gaze as intensely as if it were his hand, touching her face, her neck, glossing over her hair.

"Kate. What are you saying?"

"I'm—being pretty obvious, aren't I?"

"I'm not what you want," he said, his voice thick.

"You could be."

He took a step closer and his nostrils flared, as if he was relishing the scent of her skin, her hair, her body.

She found herself leaning in to him, the general warmth she'd felt earlier building into a specific, aching heat.

When he touched her hair, a charged sensation traveled from her scalp through all her nerve endings. "This doesn't make sense. We're adversaries. Yet around you I get this crazy impulse—"

"I feel it, too." She lifted her head, studying the depth of his blue eyes.

His hand moved from her hair to the small of her back. And then they were kissing. Lips on lips, tender and sweet.

Then he pulled back to look into her eyes.

Whatever he saw, he decided to take as encouragement, because a moment later his lips were on hers again, this time opening to her until she gasped for breath as her desire was stoked.

The second time they separated, she dropped her forehead to his chest. "Tell me this isn't crazy. Do we really want this?"

His laugh was quiet, frustrated, tense. "I can't speak for you, but it's pretty obvious from my standpoint."

She wanted to lift her head and look at him. But if she did that, she knew she would kiss him again. And maybe this time she wouldn't be able to stop at that.

"You know what I want from this?" she asked him.

His arms tightened around her back. "You want me to try and give you a baby."

She nodded, the depth of her longing so deep she could hardly breathe.

"You'll be a wonderful mother. Any child would be lucky to have you."

Was he seriously considering this? She had to risk a look at his eyes now, and they were even darker than before, like storm clouds at night.

"You should take some time to think before you make an offer like that."

"Maybe we both should."

She shook her head. All her instincts were telling her that Jay was the one. His body connected with hers in some primal, inexplicable way. He would help her make a wonderful baby. And he was at the core an honest man, one who could be trusted not to make waves, or fight her for custody afterward.

Jay touched the top button on her sweater. Gently he pulled it free. She felt the heat of his fingers on her skin, and desire flared again. Raw, aching, desperate desire, that had nothing to do with babies, and everything to do with women and men.

She lifted her face to him, and they were kissing again. No caution this time, just hungry, openmouthed kissing. His thigh pressed between her legs and she ground into him, building the ache at her core into a frantic need.

His hands slid over her hips, grabbing her derriere, pulling her closer.

You are in the office, one part of her brain reminded her. *But the office is closed. We're all alone.*

She didn't want what was happening to stop. Every touch from Jay left her craving more. He kissed her like he would possess her, then he kissed her someplace new, and the fire inside only grew hotter.

Her inner voice tried once more to protest.

Not here. Not like this.

Yet why not grasp the moment? She'd never felt so connected and attracted to a man before.

Maybe Jay wasn't husband material, but right now he seemed like the perfect man to father her child. And besides, it had to be crazy to deny this hot, delicious pleasure when they were both free and available, with no claims on their bodies or hearts.

Her sweater dropped to the floor. She'd hardly noticed him undoing the rest of the buttons. Then her bra fell and Jay was kissing her breasts. She leaned back onto the table, letting her hair fall back, opening herself to him.

He made a delicious game of removing her boots, one at a time, and then her tights, his hands running sensuously over the entire length of her legs from thighs to the tips of her toes.

And then his jeans were unzipped and she saw him swollen and fully aroused. He nudged himself up to her.

"Don't worry, Kate. Thorough medicals come with the job when you're a pilot. I'm clean."

"Me, too. And…I'm not on birth control." Her brain felt numb, but she knew she had to say that much, at least. Make sure he fully comprehended what they were doing here. It was more than just passion. At least, she hoped it would be.

He dipped his mouth to her neck, kissing her there as he slowly eased inside. Her body vibrated with pleasure and she wrapped her legs around him as she entered a zone where thoughts no longer existed.

Much later, as the blood slowly returned to her brain, she realized she was lying on the boardroom table, half-supported by Jay. She had no idea how long they had been making love, only that it had been crazily wonderful.

He stroked her hair. "You okay?"

She clung to him a moment, but the table was suddenly unbearably hard beneath her. "I'm cold."

She pulled away from him and asked for some tissues. And her sweater. Slowly they each dressed, an awkward silence between them.

"I hope—" Jay started, then stopped. "Hang on a minute."

When he returned, she was reapplying her makeup. She saw that he had cleaning supplies and without another word he washed down the table, then carefully replaced all the chairs in their proper position.

"Does that look okay?"

She nodded.

"I'm never going to feel the same way about this room again," he said. "I've even grown kind of fond of those paper clips."

She smiled as he put the supplies away, and by the time he'd returned to the conference room she was sitting in a chair, zipping up her boots.

"Kate? You're not sorry?"

"Definitely not." She met his gaze for a moment, then focused back on her boot. She wasn't sure what the rules for this situation were. They had both agreed they weren't headed for a relationship, but what she'd just shared with him felt more intimate than anything she'd ever experienced with another man.

She wondered what he was thinking right now. Probably stressing out about the repercussions of what they'd done. "Don't worry. If—if I do get pregnant, I won't ever ask anything of you. Not your money, not your time, nothing."

He flinched, as if her words hurt him. "I'd like to ask you out for dinner, but I can't. Eric will be home from basketball soon and I need to be there."

"I'm okay with that."

His smile was a little regretful. "Yeah. I see that you are. Look, Kate. I hope this…worked out. That you get what you want."

Kate stood up. She'd pulled herself together again, except for her bra, which she'd shoved into her leather bag, and she could tell Jay noticed the omission. His jaw tightened, yet he couldn't seem to tear his gaze away.

"So." He swallowed. "This it?"

"I don't know, Jay. This situation is as strange for me as I'm sure it is for you."

"We'll figure it out as we go," he said.

She nodded. There really wasn't any alternative.

CHAPTER THIRTEEN

JAY TOSSED IN HIS BED all night. He couldn't quite wrap his mind around what he'd done, which seemed crazier and crazier with each passing hour.

The trouble had started at the high school, he thought. He couldn't remember ever feeling such an overpowering jealousy before. He'd really wanted to wrap his hands around Coach Johnson's neck when the man had been flirting with Kate. He had no idea where the impulse had come from.

Then later, in the boardroom, when he and Kate were alone, she'd told him that she had zero interest in Travis Johnson. But she was interested in *him*. And that had made him feel like a million bucks.

As a teenager, he could remember times when he'd wanted sex so badly he'd have made a bargain with the devil, but as an adult—never. This was the first time in his life he'd made love without a condom. He couldn't blame Kate. She'd given him several opportunities to reconsider his decision. In the end, if he'd reached for the condom he always kept in his wallet, she would have understood.

But he hadn't. He'd made love to her with absolutely no barrier between them, and it had been unbelievably good.

And unbelievably stupid.

It wasn't that he didn't trust Kate. He knew she had no intention of involving him if she happened to get pregnant. But in his life, things had a way of going sideways, even when he thought he had all the angles covered.

He found himself imagining her pregnant.

She'd be the kind of woman who bloomed and glowed when she was expecting. And she wouldn't complain, no matter how uncomfortable or sick she felt.

Her first child would be a boy, he felt sure. But if it was a girl, wow, she'd be a cutie. Hopefully she'd have her mother's red hair and those mysterious green eyes. And freckles. Tons and tons of freckles....

But what if the girl took after *his* side of the family? What if she turned out just like his mother, and his sister, with a proclivity to addiction and a total lack of judgment where men were concerned.

He had no doubt Kate would do her best. But one day when she was halfway crazy with worry and fright, she would phone him and put the blame right where it belonged.

"You helped create this girl. Now what am I supposed to do with her?"

Jay's alarm went off suddenly, an angry buzzing sound, and he realized he'd been dreaming that Kate was yelling at him. He slammed the button to the off position, then sat up in his bed.

He took a deep breath. He had to calm down about this.

They'd only had sex one time. She probably wouldn't get pregnant. And if she did, Kate would make a terrific mother. Look how great she was with Eric. Even if she did have troubles with the kid, he would be the last person she would call for parenting help.

Jay took a shower, dressed, then knocked on Eric's door to make sure he was awake. In the kitchen he toasted waffles and poured two glasses of orange juice. As he was returning the carton to the fridge, he noticed Eric's basketball schedule.

At eight-thirty Eric finally appeared with his jacket on and backpack slung over one shoulder. He downed one of the waffles in two bites, then picked up the glass of juice.

"I see you have your first game tonight," Jay said. "I was thinking of leaving work early so I could be there."

The juice went down in one long swallow. Eric set the empty glass on the table. "Don't bother."

The rejection hit Jay in the pit of the stomach. He wasn't sure how to react. Should he be angry? Should he let Eric know that his comment had hurt?

But before he managed to get a word out, his nephew was on the move, down the hall, then out the door.

"There you are!" Nadine said as soon as Jay entered the main door of the agency.

"I'm not late, am I?" According to his watch, he was right on time.

"No, but everyone's already in the conference

room. Hannah and her husband, Jeremy, arrived ten minutes early."

Nadine handed him a cup of coffee to take in to the meeting, and he mentally prepared himself to return to the scene of the crime, as it were, and to see Kate again. He wondered if she'd had a more restful night than he had, and kind of doubted it.

She looked great, though. She was wearing a dark green sweater and she'd left her hair curly the way he liked it best, because it made her seem softer and more approachable.

Her expression was all business when she glanced at him. She was sitting at the table, right at the spot where—

"Jay, come and meet Hannah's husband, Jeremy." Nathan placed a hand on Jay's back as he made the introductions.

Jay shook hands with a slight, blond man with young-looking blue eyes. His demeanor was much more mature than his appearance, though, and his voice was deep as he said hello.

Then Jay took the only remaining chair, across from Kate.

She kept her gaze fixed on her notebook.

"Okay. Now that we're all present, we'd better get started so Jeremy and Hannah can get back to work." Lindsay, sitting at the head of the table, appeared to be chairing the meeting.

She gave him a short smile, then shot a concerned look at Kate. He wondered if Kate had talked to her about what had happened between them.

Lindsay placed her hands flat on the table and leaned slightly forward. "Kate, Jay—which of you wants to take the floor first?"

Jay hadn't made notes for the meeting, but he could see that Kate had. Almost before Lindsay stopped talking, she was speaking. Jay was partly amused, partly impressed and partly annoyed at himself for not being better prepared.

"As you know, Rebecca presented us with three possible biological fathers," Kate said in a crisp voice. "After determining that we had gathered all possible information about these men, Jay and I set out to find them. Jay, do you mind filling in Hannah and Jeremy with what we found about James Morgan?"

"Sure." He'd make this short and sweet. "James—or Jimmy as he prefers to be called—owns and manages a resort on Liberty Lake in Upper New York State. He was happy to provide a DNA sample and we just received the results of the test yesterday. They were negative."

"So he isn't my father?" Hannah looked dejected.

"No," Kate confirmed. "Which leaves us with two other possibilities.

"The first is Gary Gifford. He graduated from New England College with a degree in physical education. We were able to track him to his last place of employment, Brooklyn Heights High School. He took early retirement two years ago and we haven't been able to pick up his trail since then."

Hannah looked crushed, but Jeremy asked, "Why did he retire so early? Maybe he got cancer or something?"

"It's possible he became ill. On the plus side," Kate added, "he isn't listed on the Death Master File, so I believe he's still alive. As of today, I've got a few more leads to follow before I give up on him."

Jay wondered what those leads were. Possibly she was bluffing…but, no. That wasn't Kate's style.

"I've also located the last man on your mother's list." Kate's gaze landed briefly on Jay, and he saw a flicker of apology in her eyes. She hadn't mentioned anything about this to him, but then why should she?

He couldn't begrudge her success. While he'd had some lucky breaks, and his instincts had led him in the right direction a couple of times, he simply didn't have the investigating savvy and experience that she did.

He crossed his arms on the table and waited to hear what she had to say about prospective dad number three.

"Oliver Crane graduated with a law degree and is currently working at a practice on Park Avenue," Kate said. "He's married with two kids, and I approached him a few days ago to see if he would provide a DNA sample for testing. He refused."

Hannah drew in a quick breath and turned to her husband, who put his hand over hers. "I didn't think this was going to be so hard."

"Give them a break," Jeremy said. "They haven't been looking for long."

"And I'm not prepared to give up on Oliver Crane yet," Kate continued. "Hannah, I'd like you to write him a letter, explaining why you need to know who your father is. I'll mail it to him at his office. I also think it would help if you included some photos of you…and your mother…in with the letter."

"Put a face to the name," Lindsay murmured. "That's an excellent idea. Only a coldhearted bastard could have the heart to say no to that."

It was a good idea, Jay agreed. He noticed Nathan looking at him, encouraging him to say something, as well. But Jay had nothing to add. Kate had definitely won this round. But he wasn't ready to give up yet.

"You rock, Kate!" Lindsay gave her a high five as soon as they were alone in the conference room. Nathan had taken Hannah and Jeremy to his office so she could compose the letter that was supposed to melt Oliver Crane's heart.

As for Jay, he had quietly congratulated her, then left the office, to do what, Kate didn't know. Did he have a lead of his own?

She almost hoped that he did, which was crazy.

This job was supposed to be hers. She *deserved* this job.

"You totally owned that meeting," Lindsay continued to gloat. "Not that I ever doubted that you would come out on top."

"The competition isn't over. The case still isn't solved."

"You'll solve it. Come on. Smile. Look happy. You did great."

She should be enjoying her partial victory, Kate knew. But she couldn't help wondering what Jay had been thinking about during the meeting. His mind had been someplace else, that was for sure.

Was he sorry about what they'd done yesterday? She really hoped not. She'd have to be very careful to live up to her side of the bargain, to make no demands on him, to make him believe that she really wanted no more from him than that one very hot, very sweaty moment.

And a baby.

It was possible it could happen. She'd checked her calendar at home last night and she was at the right point in her cycle. Of course there were no guarantees. She'd heard of couples who had tried for months, sometimes a year or more.

"So what was up with you and Jay?" Lindsay asked, lowering her voice. "He hardly took his eyes off you all meeting. I don't think it had anything to do with the case."

"You're imagining things." She wasn't going to tell her friend what they had done. Later, if she found out she was pregnant…maybe.

"Hey, girls, it's too soon for a victory party yet," Nathan said, coming in the room with the letter from Hannah. He gave it to her with a nod of approval. "Impressive work, Kate. Well done."

It was a measure of his character that he was rising above his personal bias for Jay to win this contest, and Kate thanked him. Then she glanced over the letter.

"This sounds good."

"Hannah's going to e-mail you some pictures when she gets back to her office," Nathan said. "So you can include them in the package. If this doesn't melt Oliver Crane's heart, I don't know what will."

"Thanks, Nathan. I'll make sure he receives this

today. I could tell Hannah and Jeremy were disappointed we hadn't found her father yet."

"Seemed to me that Hannah was more disappointed than Jeremy. Still, the sooner we get this resolved, the sooner Lindsay and I can start dumping more work on someone else's shoulders."

Kate smiled. "I hope they'll be mine."

Nathan hesitated. "May the best person win, Kate. That's all I can say."

KATE WAITED FOR HANNAH'S e-mail, then she printed out the pictures and enclosed them in an envelope with the letter Hannah had written for Oliver Crane. It was a good, heartfelt plea, and as Nathan had said, only someone without a heart could fail to be moved by it. She addressed the envelope and was about to give it to Nadine to send by courier, when she realized it would arrive much faster if she delivered it in person.

On her way out of the office she met up with Lindsay, who was also getting her coat from the closet.

"I need to buy some more toys for the kids at the shelter," Lindsay explained. They both volunteered at the Women's Emergency Shelter. Lindsay liked to make sure that each child who booked into the home was given a brand-new toy of their own, whereas Kate taught a class on self-defense the fourth Wednesday of every month.

Lindsay and Kate walked together as far as the toy store. Lindsay talked about the deluge of cases that she hoped Kate would help her with once she was officially on staff at Fox & Fisher.

"I appreciate your confidence, but I'm not so sure Jay won't solve this case first. He doesn't have my training and experience but he has amazing instincts about people."

"So do you. I like Jay, too. I wish we could hire you both. But right now all we need is one employee. So if I were you, I'd concentrate on being the one and stop talking about how good Jay is."

They parted at the toy store, and Kate continued toward the Park Avenue address, her thoughts on her conversation with Lindsay. Her friend was right. She talked about Jay too much. She thought about him too much also.

After what had happened between them yesterday, it was important that she treat him in a purely professional way. She'd made him a promise and she had to live up to it.

But it wouldn't be easy. She'd felt so different around him this morning. She wasn't surprised Lindsay had picked up on the vibes between them.

And she'd thought about him a lot last night. She'd thought about the baby, too, but even more about Jay, which wasn't right. She realized she had some regrets of her own.

One was that due to the circumstances they'd found themselves in—mainly making love on a boardroom table—they'd had no opportunity to cuddle and talk after.

Also, she wished that they could have gone for dinner together. Not a date. They didn't have that sort of a relationship. But just a chance to talk and get adjusted to the shift in their…relationship.

When she reached Crane's law office, Kate told herself she simply had to stop thinking about Jay. This was work and it was important. She took the elevator to the fifteenth floor, then approached the understated yet elegant reception desk.

"I have a letter for Oliver Crane that I'd like to deliver in person."

An attractive, stylishly dressed and coiffed receptionist peered over dark-framed glasses and held out her hand. "I'll make sure he gets the letter."

"I'd prefer to deliver it in person."

She frowned. "Is this a subpoena?"

"No."

"Well. Mr. Crane's next appointment is in twenty minutes. If you take a seat over there, you'll be able to catch him on his way out."

Kate made her way to the designated seating area, resigned to the wait. She picked up the front section of the *New York Times* and scanned the dire headlines. Some people questioned the wisdom of bringing more children into this messed-up world. But Kate couldn't buy into that theory. There was still hope, she sincerely believed, that the world could become a better place.

Fifteen minutes later, Kate had finished with the paper and was replacing it on the coffee table, when Oliver Crane appeared in the hall wearing a dark blue wool jacket and carrying a briefcase. He stopped to talk to the receptionist, and they both glanced at her.

Oliver Crane's nose wrinkled as if he'd just caught scent of a foul odor.

She stood and headed toward him. Without saying a word, she held out the envelope.

He regarded it suspiciously, then lifted his gaze back to her.

"It's from Hannah Young," she said. "Please read it."

He stood frozen for several moments. Then finally he gave a short nod and accepted the envelope. Without uttering a word, not a promise or another denial, he continued on his way out of the building.

AFTER THE CLIENT MEETING, Jay left the office on a hunt for a cab. When he flagged one down, he jumped into the backseat. "Brooklyn Heights High School."

He had a need for action now. Movement. Progress.

Kate had impressed the hell out of him at that meeting, proving yet again that she was every bit as intelligent as she was beautiful. He couldn't believe she'd already located and met with Oliver Crane. Now that she had that letter from Hannah, it was only a matter of time before she convinced the lawyer to provide a DNA sample.

Which meant his only chance to come out on top was to find Gary Gifford before she did.

Yesterday, Coach Johnson had mentioned something about Gifford being sweet on one of the teachers. He'd claimed not to know which teacher, but someone at that school had to be in on the secret. Jay wanted to find that woman and talk to her. If anyone would know why Gary had taken early retirement, surely she would.

The taxi pulled up to the school just before noon. Jay checked in at reception and found the school secretary as frosty as she'd been the previous day. He stood in front of her desk for several minutes—while she shuffled papers around—before she finally acknowledged him.

"Hello," he said. "It's Jay Savage from Fox & Fisher again."

"I see that." Her lips pinched in a frown as if daring him to come up with a good reason for disturbing her *this time*.

Jay took a deep breath. Maybe she hated her job. Maybe she was having personal problems at home. But at heart, she was probably a kind person.

"I'm sorry to bother you again. This is a big school and you must be very busy. But it's important that I find Coach Gifford. I have news that could change his life."

The secretary's eyes widened. He thought, hoped, he'd managed to intrigue her.

He leaned in closer to her and lowered his voice. "Yesterday Coach Johnson told me that Gifford had been sweet on one of the staff members. In your position, I figure you see a lot of things. Know a lot of things. Do you think you could point me in the right direction?"

She put her hand to her throat as she considered his words. Then she nodded. "I don't believe in passing along gossip. But if you talk to Lillian Price—she's the music teacher—she may be able to help you."

"Thank you." He gave her a broad smile. "Thank you very much."

"Turn right when you leave here, then go down the hall to your left. The music room is at the far end. You'll see a sign."

"Right."

"Coach Gifford was a lonely man," she said. "I hope you're bringing him good news."

Jay wasn't so sure about that. Gary Gifford had never married, never had children. Presumably he'd had a reason. Maybe, like Jay, he'd never wanted the responsibility.

So how could he possibly be happy to find out that he had a twenty-five-year-old daughter?

Still, Hannah had a right to this information, Jay believed, and it was his job to find out the truth on her behalf.

As he was making his way along the corridors, the buzzer signaling lunch break sounded. Within seconds, he was wading through a mass of teenage bodies. Finally free of the constraints of the classroom, they exploded with energy—laughing, talking, calling out to one another.

"I'll meet you in the parking lot—"

"Wasn't that boring?"

"Where's Sarah? I told her we would wait for her."

His height was a definite advantage as he worked his way through the crosscurrents of teenagers moving in every possible direction. Finally he was at the end of the hall. A brass doorplate identified the room to his left as the music hall. He waited until the last student had left before making his way in.

A small woman, probably in her early forties, and wearing a peach-colored sweater, was closing the lid on the piano. She glanced up when she noticed him, and her cheeks turned the color of her sweater. She'd been in the staff room when he'd made his appeal, asking if anyone had kept in touch with Coach Gifford.

She hadn't said anything then, and his hopes sank a little. Still, maybe she'd be more forthcoming in private.

"I'm Jay Savage from The Fox & Fisher Detective Agency."

She glanced down at her hands. "I remember."

"When I was talking to Coach Johnson, he mentioned that Gary Gifford had a crush on one of the teachers in the school. I was wondering if you knew anything about that?"

She swallowed and her cheeks grew a deeper shade of pink. She got up from the piano bench and went to close the door.

"I'm married," she said. "I've been married for thirteen years."

The room was silent for a long while as he processed what she was telling him.

"I understand," he said finally. "I intend to be completely discreet. I just want to find Gary. That's all."

"I don't know where he is. When he found out he was sick, he took it very hard. Probably because he was used to being athletic and strong, he couldn't deal with the prospect of becoming wheelchair-bound."

"What was wrong with him?"

"I think I noticed the changes in him before he did. He was usually so focused and decisive. But he started forgetting things and acting befuddled. Plus he was getting clumsy. Even his students noticed that. I convinced him to go to the doctor."

"And what did they tell him?"

Lillian Price seemed suddenly smaller and sadder. Lines of sorrow pulled on her eyes, her mouth.

"They told him he had Huntington's."

Jay knew a little about the disease. He knew it affected a person's mind and body. That it was degenerative and eventually fatal.

"The diagnosis as good as killed him. He cut off all ties with anyone who cared about him."

"Including you?"

She nodded. "He said he wanted me to remember him the way he was."

"So he put in for early retirement. And then what?"

"I have no idea." She raised her palms despairingly. "I was married. I couldn't—"

"I understand." He felt badly for her, and for Gary Gifford. "What a lousy break."

She nodded. "That's why I didn't say anything to you yesterday. There was no point. I can't help you find Gary. I only wish I could. But—if you find him…"

"Yes?"

"Tell him hello from me. Tell him… Just tell him hello."

CHAPTER FOURTEEN

JAY LEFT THE SCHOOL wondering about Gary Gifford. What kind of man had he been? Most people turned to those they loved in times of trouble. But Gary had gone the opposite way, becoming a virtual recluse after his diagnosis. Had he really wanted to preserve his memory in the hearts of the people he cared about? Or had he wanted to spare them the pain and unhappiness of watching him slowly disintegrate until he died?

Either way made for a tragic tale.

And, either way, he still had no clue where Gary was now. Not dead, Kate claimed, based on her research. So then where could he be?

Jay had really been hoping this lead would take him somewhere. But he was no further ahead now than he'd been this morning.

And then there was Kate.

She was still in his mind. No matter what he did or tried to focus on, he couldn't get her to budge.

He remembered the panicked feeling from his dream and knew he had to talk to her before the day was through.

As he waited for a taxi to pick him up, he found himself dialing her cell phone.

"Jay? What's up?"

"I was thinking— I wondered if you'd like to meet for a late lunch. I should be back around two."

A yellow cab turned a corner and Jay raised his hand. The cab slowed, then stopped, and Jay climbed inside.

"Manhattan," he said, giving the address of the office.

"Back?" Kate asked. "From where?"

"Just following up on a lead…" He'd let her think he was making progress, though the opposite was true.

"Okay. I'll meet you for lunch. The Stool Pigeon okay?"

"Well, at least it's convenient."

She laughed. "Yes. We can give it that much."

JAY WAS WAITING FOR HER when Kate walked into the pub. As soon as he saw her, he stood, and she felt a champagne pop of joy as he smiled at her.

She had no idea why he'd asked her to lunch. All she knew was that she'd wanted to see him, so she'd said yes. This probably wasn't the smartest thing she'd ever done, but for now, she was going on instinct.

She headed for his booth, tossing down her leather case before sliding onto the vinyl bench across from him.

"So, how was your morning? You took off quickly after our client meeting."

"I had some catching up to do." He tipped his glass of water in salute. "I had no idea you'd already found Oliver Crane."

She smiled ruefully. "Yes, I found him. Fat lot of good it's done me, though."

"I presume you've sent him Hannah's letter?"

"I delivered it this morning, in person. I'm not too hopeful it'll penetrate that heart of his. I'm guessing it's made of titanium."

Wendy approached to take their sandwich orders. She frowned when they both requested salads rather than fries for their sides. "You only live once," she told them.

"We don't all have Lindsay's metabolism," Kate countered. She waited until Wendy had moved on to another table before leaning closer to Jay. "Your turn. What have you been up to this morning?"

"Kate, Kate, Kate…you've already got the advantage on me. It's not fair for you to charm me out of my secrets."

"So you *were* working on the case?"

"Sure. But that's not why I wanted to have lunch."

Something in his expression warned her this wasn't going to be good news. "You're sorry, aren't you?"

"Not about what happened. About the *way* it happened. Kate, I've never had unprotected sex before."

How could he be saying this to her now? This wasn't fair. "I asked you—"

"I know. You gave me plenty of chances to back out. I'm not saying I'm not responsible. I just want you to know that if—if it doesn't work out, then I'm sorry, but that's it."

"No more stud service?" she asked bitterly.

"God. This isn't coming out right."

"I think it's coming out exactly the way you mean it."

He reached for her hand, but she pulled it off the table.

"I tried to tell you from the beginning, you should be going for the whole package. For a man who has a lot more to offer than me."

"What are you really afraid of?" she asked.

"Nothing. Stop trying to twist my words. I don't want children. I was always up-front about that."

"And I was up-front, too," she reminded him. "If I'm pregnant, if I'm lucky enough to have a baby, I am going to love this child so much. I'll be the very best mother I can possibly be."

She got up from the table, no longer interested in food of any variety. "You are off the hook, Jay. In fact, you were never on one."

WHEN WENDY BROUGHT the salads to the table, she didn't seem surprised to find him alone. Maybe this sort of thing happened regularly at the Stool Pigeon. Jay didn't know. He really didn't care. He'd thought he'd feel better after his conversation with Kate. Being honest and up-front with the women he slept with had always worked for him before. But this time, he felt worse.

It didn't help that nothing else in his life was going right. He kept hitting walls with the case, and Eric didn't even want him to watch his basketball game.

Jay took his lunch and went to sit at the bar. March Madness was playing on the TV. Not his favorite tournament to watch, but the guy sitting two stools over seemed to be captivated.

"My son plays basketball better than these guys," he complained to Jay.

Jay glanced over at the guy, who was probably five years older than him, dressed in a suit, his PDA on the counter beside his plate of fish and chips. "Yeah? Do you watch his games?"

"As many as I can." He broke off a piece of his deep-fried halibut with a fork. "You got kids?"

"My nephew lives with me. He just started playing basketball. His first game's today. But he told me he didn't want me to come."

"How old is he?"

"Fourteen."

"If I was you, I'd go to the game."

"You think?"

"Teenagers are like women. They never say what they really want. With women, it's because they think you should *know* without them having to say anything. With teenagers, it's because they're bloody clueless."

JAY DECIDED TO TAKE THE stranger's advice and go to Eric's basketball game. Maybe if he sat high in the bleachers his nephew wouldn't even notice him.

The girls were just finishing up their game when Jay arrived at the school gymnasium. He climbed up and took a seat above most of the other spectators, a couple dozen parents, family and friends.

Anxiously he waited to see if Eric would spot him. When he did, Jay was surprised to see a little smile on the boy's face. But it was soon replaced with a frown of concentration.

There was plenty of sloppy play in the beginning. Eric threw a bounce pass a few feet from anyone on either side and it went out of bounds. Dejected, Eric returned to the bench.

His play improved in the third quarter, though, when he scored two points to help the Raiders extend their lead to 24-16.

Jay was pleased that Eric was given a fair amount of time on the court. Despite his uneven play, Jay could see that he had a natural sense of balance and hand-eye co-ordination. With practice he could become one of the better players.

After the game, Jay waited for Eric to shower and change and they traveled home together.

For once conversation came easily as they went over a play-by-play analysis of the game. Jay made sure to make only encouraging comments, not focusing on the things Eric had done wrong.

They stopped at the market on the way home and bought steaks, potatoes and vegetables. When Eric complained, Jay said, "Trust me. You'll like this way better than pepperoni-and-cheese pizza."

When the meal was ready, Eric didn't make a stink about sitting at the table to eat. From the way he attacked the steak, he'd gotten over the fact that they hadn't ordered pizza.

Suddenly Jay remembered another of Eric's favorite foods. "Do you still like hot dogs?"

"Yeah. Why?"

"I remember taking you to your first Yankees game." He'd bought Eric a cap and the boy had worn it proudly for about two years. "You loved it. And I've never seen a kid eat more hot dogs."

Eric froze. Then he swallowed. "That was a long time ago." He finished his last piece of steak, then got up from the table, leaving the vegetables on his plate untouched.

Jay wondered what he'd said wrong this time. He cleared the table and loaded the dishwasher. There was no sound coming from Eric's room. He was probably listening to his iPod again. Sighing, Jay dried his hands, then headed to Eric's room. He knocked on the door.

"May I come in?"

No answer.

He pushed on the door and it swung inward a few inches. "Eric? I'd like to talk to you."

Eric was sitting on the bed, with his back against the wall. He'd pulled on his wool cap and he was listening to his music with his eyes closed.

Jay sat on the mattress beside him. He waited until Eric unplugged one of his ears.

"We used to do a lot of things together when you were younger," Jay started, feeling his way into the conversation. When Eric nodded, he took that as a positive sign.

"Your mom used to ask me to babysit quite often. I never minded. I loved hanging out with you, whenever I wasn't working."

Eric said nothing, but he was clearly listening, so Jay continued.

"Then when you were eleven or twelve, your mom decided you didn't need babysitting anymore. After that, I didn't hear from her much. Especially not after she started seeing that last boyfriend of hers—"

"Steve."

"Yeah, Steve. To be honest, I'd never liked any of your mother's boyfriends, but I really didn't like Steve." Tracy's usual choice in men was lazy, dumb and needy. Steve had been worse. He'd actually been dishonest.

Jay had checked into his past and discovered he had a criminal record. When he told Tracy, had she thanked him? Oh, no, she'd been furious and had insisted he butt out of her life.

"I didn't like Steve, either. He was mean."

Jay tensed. "Did he ever hurt you?"

"Not me. But Mom, sometimes."

Hell. Guilt gnawed at Jay's gut.

Almost two years had passed, Jay realized, between the time he'd last seen Eric and his mom's death. Two years could pass by pretty quickly for an adult. But for a kid, it must have seemed a long, long time.

Eric must have thought he'd deserted him.

In a way he had.

"I'm sorry I slipped out of your life there for a while. And I'm really sorry I wasn't around when you and your mom needed me the most."

Tentatively, Jay put his arm around his nephew's shoulders. He wasn't used to touching other men. He'd never had a father or uncles. Eric felt stiff and unyield-ing, but he left his arm there anyway.

Tracy had been a great one for hugging, like their mother. He bet that was something Eric missed.

"I guess I sucked at being your uncle for a few years, huh?"

Eric said nothing, but his eyes were glistening with tears. Jay could feel his own eyes welling up. "But I'm here now, and I'm not going anywhere this time."

KATE LAY IN BED the next morning, her hands on her tummy. Nothing felt different, but it was probably too soon for that. She tried to picture a miracle happening inside of her. Cells dividing, new life growing.

If wishing could make it happen, then she would be pregnant for sure.

But she was almost positive she wasn't. No one got pregnant the first time unless they didn't want to. It was one of Murphy's laws.

And there sure wasn't going to be a second time.

To hell with Jay and his regrets. She wasn't sorry they'd made love, and she certainly wasn't sorry they hadn't used birth control.

At the office, Nadine was on the phone with her mother. Kate could tell by her voice, and by her posture, not to mention the subject of the conversation.

"Yes, I went with Robbie to Eileen's charity gala, but we're not serious. Of course I'd tell you if we were."

Kate gave her a sympathetic smile as she waited.

When Nadine covered the mouthpiece and cocked her head, Kate spoke quickly.

"Any calls? I was hoping I might hear from Oliver Crane."

"Sorry. No." Nadine went back to listening to her mother and Kate carried on to her office, slipping into her chair and powering up the computer.

She considered her options.

Yesterday she'd delivered Hannah's letter to Oliver Crane, along with the Fox & Fisher phone number and e-mail. But Crane hadn't been in touch or left a message.

Had Hannah's letter failed to move him?

Maybe he needed more time. At any rate, she couldn't think of anything more she could do to persuade him to give them a DNA sample, other than follow him to the gym again and steal a sample of his hair. She really hoped it didn't come down to that.

Today she'd have to focus on finding Coach Gifford.

Kate went to get a glass of water. Nadine was still on the phone, rolling her eyes now.

"Mom, I really need to get to work, okay? I promise if Robbie asks me to marry him on our second date, I'll let you know." She hung up the phone and apologized to Kate. "Too bad Fox & Fisher can't have an unlisted number. Though, even if they did, my mom would find me somehow."

"She's anxious to marry you off?"

"She didn't used to be. But that was before I decided I wanted to be a private investigator. Now she imagines I spend my days dodging bullets and cavorting with the

Mafia and she seems to think the only thing that will save me is to walk down a church aisle in ivory-colored silk and Italian lace."

Kate laughed, then returned to her office and closed the door. She needed quiet to think.

What did she know about Gary Gifford? She opened her notebook and reviewed all the facts she had so far. The trail ended with his early retirement from Brooklyn Heights High School, at the age of forty-two. Why had he left his job so young? That was the question that she had to answer.

She jotted down possible reasons. Maybe he had received an inheritance and had decided to go travel-ing. If so, he could be anywhere in the world right now.

Why else would someone retire early? Johnson had suggested a health issue, but that could be anything. She didn't think it was life-threatening, because his death wasn't listed. But maybe he'd contracted something that had made it impossible for him to continue coach-ing. The man had no wife or kids. In a case like that, what would he do? Maybe check into some sort of long-term-care facility?

Kate pulled up a map of Brooklyn and identified every assisted-living and full-care residence within an eight-mile radius of Gifford's home and the school where he'd worked.

Once she had a list, she methodically worked her way through the phone numbers. After about an hour, her hunch paid off.

"Yes, we have a Mr. Gary Gifford living with us. Are you a former student of his?"

Kate hesitated only a second before leaving her real name. "I'm Kate Cooper."

"I'll have to see if he remembers you. He has his good days and his bad days. But in any case, Coach Gifford is very selective about visitors."

"Please do ask," Kate said. "I'll call back later and see if it's okay for me to visit." She hung up, intending to do nothing of the kind. Unless Coach Gifford's problem was early onset dementia, no way was he going to remember a student named Kate Cooper.

She'd need to find some other way to gain admittance to his room, and the best way to do that was to find out everything possible about Maple Ridge Assisted Living, then check out the place in person.

She plugged into the Internet first, and found a Web site that very usefully included a floor plan for the three-story structure. She printed that, then clicked on the directions tab for a map to the nursing home. When that came up on her screen, she hit Print again.

Nothing happened this time. Darn—the printer was out of paper.

Sighing, she found an unused sheet on her desk and stuck it in the tray. Impatiently, she hit the print command one more time, and five seconds later the machine spewed out what she needed.

She stuffed all her papers into her leather bag and headed for the exit.

She didn't tell Nadine where she was going. Not that

she didn't trust the young receptionist, but she didn't want her to inadvertently tip Jay off on Gary Gifford's location.

With any luck, this was going to be the lead that finally solved the case.

CHAPTER FIFTEEN

"HOW ARE YOU, KATE?" Jay had been prepared to run into her. But not here on the street in front of the agency, he on his way in, she obviously heading out.

She looked great, he thought, in her long, gray cable-knit sweater over black tights and suede boots. Though he preferred her hair natural and curly, he had to admit it looked terrific when she wore it straight, the way she was today. The color seemed richer, the texture glossy, inviting his touch.

He was reminded of his impression the first time he'd met her, that here was a woman who was fashion-model beautiful on the outside, but cold and calculating within.

Now he knew that was far from the truth. Kate was beautiful inside and out. She could be coolly analytical when it came to her job. But show her a friend in need, or a child in trouble, and she was there.

She tightened her sweater around her body, as if she had something to conceal from him. Though it was illogical, he found himself checking out her still-slim waistline.

"I'm fine. How is Eric?"

"He had his first basketball game yesterday. He did well." There was so much more he wanted to share with her. But he could tell from her eyes that she was still wounded by what he'd said yesterday.

"And he's going to school?"

"As far as I can tell." At least there'd been no more phone calls from the TRACK program.

"Okay, well, I'd better get going."

"Did Oliver Crane crack?" He couldn't stop himself from asking, even though she was under no obligation to share her information.

"Afraid not."

So she must have a lead on Gary Gifford.

"Look, Jay, I have to run."

She hitched her sweater tightly around her middle again, then turned and started walking toward Columbia Street. He kept standing there until she had turned the corner.

NADINE LOOKED UP with a smile when she saw Jay. "You just missed Kate."

"I know. I saw her outside on the stairs."

"You guys are coming and going so much, it's hard to keep track of everyone." Nadine made a notation on her calendar, then asked if he'd like some fresh coffee.

"That would be great."

"It'll be ready in a minute," she promised him.

"Thanks. I need the caffeine."

He needed something to jump-start his thinking process, he thought as he made his way to their shared office. Kate may have left the premises, but he could still smell her perfume. He inhaled a few times, the scent bringing back memories of how it had felt to have her in his arms.

Their time together had been short but unforgettable. He sighed as he sank into his chair. He opened his laptop and began typing up his notes from his meeting with Lillian yesterday.

Had she said anything significant that he'd missed?

If only she'd kept in touch with Gary somehow. But he didn't doubt that she'd been telling him the truth…. Her pain had been too authentic.

Jay leaned back in his chair and thought about Gary. He'd been only ten years older than him, unmarried and childless, working at a job he loved, when he'd found out he had a degenerative disease.

The disease had forced him to quit the job that had been the focus of his life. Even worse, he would no longer have an excuse to spend time with the woman he loved but could never have.

What was the logical course of action for Gary to take in a situation like that?

What would *he* do in Gary's shoes?

Well, for starters, he would probably move. And that got Jay thinking about another thing—Gary must have had neighbors. Maybe *they* knew what had happened to him. Did he have Gary's last known address in his notes?

Nadine tapped on the door and came in with his coffee. She set the mug on the corner of his desk.

"You are the sweetest woman." He took a gulp, then

scrolled through his background notes on Gary. There was the address. He decided to print it out and head over right away.

After connecting the cable from his laptop to the office printer, he hit the command button, only to realize the printer was out of paper.

He had no idea where to find paper, so he went to ask Nadine, who kindly gave him a big stack. As soon as he'd filled the tray, the printer starting working.

It wasn't his document that came out first, though, but directions to a nursing home. Jay picked up the piece of paper and stared at it.

After a few seconds, the significance sunk in.

This was where Kate had been rushing off to when he'd passed her on the stairs. She'd found Coach Gifford in a nursing home.

JAY SLIPPED ON his sunglasses as he stepped out to the street, searching for a cab.

The day was bright, the air calm. Perfect winter flying weather. He felt the old yearning and flexed his hands, remembering the feel of the controls from his cargo pilot days—his first job after flight school.

He'd seen some beautiful, awe-inspiring sights back then. Snow-covered mountain ranges, ice-blue skies and acres and acres of evergreen forests. He could fly for hours without any sign of human life below.

He'd loved that job, and had only quit when he heard his mother was sick and not expected to last long. And she hadn't. Six months after he'd relocated to Manhattan, his mother was buried and he was trying to get his sister into a rehab program for her meth addiction.

Those had been the pre-Eric days. When Tracy had realized she was pregnant, she'd turned her life around for a while. For a glorious period of two or three years, she'd devoted herself to being a mother...until the next jerk walked into her life and messed her head up all over again.

A cab stopped and Jay hurried inside, giving brief instructions to the driver then sinking back to watch the constant stream of passing buildings.

Jay closed his eyes. The pace of the past few months was catching up to him. The brief exhilaration he'd felt a moment ago had passed and now he was engulfed with a sense of profound sadness. For his sister. For Eric. Even for a man he'd never known and the woman who had loved him, but been unable to help him when he'd found out he was dying.

Snap out of this, he finally told himself. There was nothing to be gained by letting the past bog him down. He thought about Kate—she had about thirty minutes on him. Perhaps she wouldn't even be at the nursing home when he arrived. For all he knew, right this moment she was on her way to BioFinds Lab with a sample of Gary's DNA.

"Here you are," the driver said, pulling to a stop about fifteen minutes later. Jay paid him, then stepped out to the street.

The Brooklyn Heights nursing home was a redbrick, three-story structure built in a *U* shape, with a garden in the center. Paved paths meandered through the shrubs, and benches were placed at discreet intervals. It was much too cold for anyone to be sitting out there now, of course, but the paths had been cleared of snow, and a couple of chickadees were fighting over a seed feeder strung from a branch of one of the taller shrubs.

All in all, it did not seem an unattractive place to live out your final years, Jay thought. If someone was paying attention to details outdoors, hopefully the same was taking place inside with the residents.

He made his way through the automatically opening glass-fronted doors and was surprised to see Kate standing in the waiting area, talking on her cell phone. She was focused on the call and hadn't noticed him.

He wondered why she hadn't left for the lab. Maybe she still hadn't spoken to Gary Gifford. Was it possible he could get the sample before she did?

Jay scrubbed his feet on the rubber matt by the door, then approached the receptionist. Whether Kate had seen him already or not, he still wanted to meet Gary Gifford. If nothing else, he really should pass along Lillian Price's greeting.

The receptionist was in her fifties, with short curly hair and glasses, and she sat behind a high counter topped with granite and protected with a sliding glass partition.

She looked at him curiously. "I'll be right with you." Then she returned her attention to a young man in a nursing uniform standing by her side with a clipboard.

Meanwhile, Kate was ending her call. "If it's okay with you, I'll go ahead and ask him. I'll phone you right back and let you know what he says."

She snapped her phone shut and slid it into the front pocket of her sweater. Then she saw Jay.

Her mouth dropped open, then her jaw tightened and her eyes narrowed. She moved toward him. "I don't believe this."

"Just can't shake me, can you? Still, you found Gary Gifford first. Congratulations."

"What are you doing here? How did you possibly—" She shook her head. "I keep underestimating you."

He thought guiltily of the directions spewed out by the printer, but didn't mention anything about that. He could salvage his pride a little and pretend he hadn't been that far behind.

"So do you have the sample?" he asked.

She frowned, annoyed. "Gary Gifford won't talk to me."

"Why not?"

"Apparently he's a bit of a recluse. According to the head nurse, he only has one regular visitor. A former student from his coaching days."

This was an unforeseen complication. "So now what?"

"I wondered if he might remember Rebecca. I just got off the phone with her. She says she'll drive over here if we can get him to agree to talk to her."

"Smart plan."

Kate took a deep breath. "Here's hoping it works."

Jay hung back as she went to talk to the woman at reception. After a few minutes, a nurse came out to join the discussion. She listened to Kate, nodded, then went back, presumably to relay the message to Gary Gifford.

Jay went to stand with Kate at that point. She had her arms crossed over her middle and her features were set tensely. "So close," she murmured. "So close. Please let him say yes."

But when the nurse finally returned, she was shaking her head. "I'm sorry, Ms. Cooper, but Mr. Gifford doesn't want to see his old college friend, either. I'm afraid he's very sensitive about his physical condition."

"Maybe another letter from Hannah," Jay suggested. They'd tried that approach with Oliver Crane. Why not with Coach Gifford?

"This is so frustrating. We're so close..." Kate thanked the nurse and the receptionist for their help, then went to retrieve her coat from a rack by the entrance.

"You're giving up?" he asked, surprised to see that she seemed to be about to leave.

"I can't think of anything else to do...." She shrugged. "Maybe I will ask Hannah for another letter. Though, frankly, I'll be very surprised if Gary Gifford even reads it."

Jay couldn't help but feel badly for Kate's setback. She'd been smart and she'd worked hard.

"You deserved a better outcome," he told her.

"I'll figure something out yet."

He nodded. She wasn't the type to give up. "Want me to call you a cab?"

She seemed surprised. "I thought we would share—"

"I'm going to hang around a bit longer."

Her eyes narrowed suspiciously, but before she could ask him why, her phone rang.

"Kate Cooper," she said in a flat, businesslike tone. A few seconds later, her eyes brightened. "Really? You bet I'll come. I'll be there as quickly as possible."

He waited, but she didn't explain who had called or where she was headed next.

"See you later, Jay."

"Good luck," he called after her.

She turned then, and met his gaze squarely. "You, too," she said, and then she was gone.

Jay shoved his hands into his pockets and tried to come up with a plan. It was crazy to be this close to Gary Gifford, only to be turned away.

Finally he approached the receptionist, who wore a badge that read Shelby Summers.

"Excuse me, Ms. Summers, I was just wondering... Kate said Mr. Gifford has an ex-student who visits him every week?"

"Yes. Marc Certosimo is a wonderful young man."

"Can you tell me when he usually comes?"

She glanced at the calendar on her desk. "Why, today. But not until later in the evening. Usually some time after seven."

"Thanks." Jay smiled. It seemed luck was on his side again.

HANNAH'S LETTER TO Oliver Crane had been effective after all. The Park Avenue lawyer met Kate at the juice bar by his gym. He had a wool coat over his designer suit, and a burgundy silk scarf around his neck. He would have looked quite sharp, however his ears added a slightly comic touch. In clipped, businesslike tones, he asked her what he needed to do in order to provide an appropriate DNA sample.

She gave him the kit, he took it to the washroom, and was back five minutes later. She held out her hand, but Crane still had one condition.

"I'm providing this sample with the proviso that no one—not you, or anyone from your agency, and especially not Hannah—contacts me again."

"But when we get the results—"

"I don't want to know about them. You can tell your client that if it turns out I am her biological father, then she should consider it a pretty clean bill of health. My father had a heart attack in his sixties, but he was an overweight smoker who never exercised."

A pattern his son had definitely not followed, Kate thought. Judging by his trim physique, he did more at his gym than sip carrot juice at the fruit bar.

"There are no other health issues that I'm aware of," he told her. Then he set the bag with his DNA sample on the table. "Now, do I have your word that my privacy will be respected?"

She couldn't stop herself from asking, "But aren't you curious?"

His gray eyes flashed impatiently. "I could give you ten very good reasons why I shouldn't provide you with this sample. I have career aspirations beyond the legal profession and I have no desire to have illegitimate children popping out of the woodwork."

"Hannah has agreed to keep the results absolutely

confidential. I'm sure she'll also agree never to contact you again, if that really is your wish."

"It is." He shook her hand then, and finally passed over the DNA sample.

As Kate watched him leave, it occurred to her that what she found so unbelievable in Oliver Crane—that he could walk away from his own biological child with such apparent ease—was exactly what she had asked Jay to do.

AT A QUARTER TO SEVEN, JAY returned to the nursing home. Someone new was sitting at the reception desk now. As he approached, he squinted to read her badge. Rosie McBride looked close to retirement, with silver curls and penciled-in eyebrows.

"May I help you?" she asked cheerfully.

"I hope so." He explained that he was waiting for Marc Certosimo, and that he would appreciate it if she would point him out when he arrived for his usual visit.

"No need for Rosie to do that," a strong, young voice said from behind him.

He turned to see a muscle-bound man in his early twenties, dressed in a training suit and wearing white sneakers that made his feet look clownishly large.

"I'm Marc Certosimo."

"Glad to meet you. Jay Savage." He offered a hand, which the young man proceeded to crush in a grip that went beyond firm.

"Is this about Coach Gifford?"

Given the setting, it was a logical question, and Jay nodded. "Can we sit down and talk for a minute?"

"If it doesn't take too long." Marc followed him to the reception area, then lowered his body into one of the chairs.

Jay didn't often meet men who were his size, and Marc was slightly bigger. He leaned forward in his seat and made eye contact, hoping to establish a rapport.

"You play football?"

"Defensive end for New England College."

"Coach Gifford's alma mater."

"That's right." A gleam of respect showed in the kid's eyes. "You're too old to be one of his students. How do you know the coach?"

"I'm working on behalf of The Fox & Fisher Detective Agency in Manhattan. One of their clients believes Coach Gifford could be her father."

"No shit? What makes her think that?"

"Her mother had a thing with Coach Gifford in their first year of college," Jay said, tactfully refraining from referring to the encounter as a one-night stand.

"Is that right?" Marc grinned. "So the coach had a girlfriend in his past. Cool. Most of the guys at school figured he was gay."

"Not you?"

"I could tell he was crazy about our high school music teacher, Lillian Price. They went kind of gaga when they were in the same room together. But she was married, and the coach wasn't the kind of guy to get in the way of that."

"So you would call him an honorable man?" Jay hoped he had finally found his opening.

"Definitely."

"Then you would think that if he had fathered a child, he would be willing to own up to it."

Marc's eyes widened at Jay's bluntness, but he took a minute to reflect, then nodded. "Yeah. I think he would. But if his daughter is hoping to squeeze some money out of him, tell her to forget it. All his pension goes toward this place."

"This isn't about money," Jay assured him. "His daughter is planning to have a baby. Huntington's is a genetic disease. If she's his daughter, then she has a right to know if she's a carrier."

"Hell," Marc said. "That's for sure."

"Someone else working for the agency, Kate Cooper, was here earlier. She asked Mr. Gifford if he would provide a DNA sample for testing. It's a simple procedure—all we need is saliva from his mouth—but he refused."

"Maybe he didn't understand the request. He has his good days and his bad days, if you know what I mean."

"Would you mind bringing it up with him?"

"I don't see what it could hurt. I'll talk to him."

"Here." Jay passed him one of the test kits. "If he agrees, you can get the sample right away. Like I said, it's really easy to do."

Marc turned to leave, then Jay called him back.

"One more thing. Would you tell him that Lillian Price says hello?"

CHAPTER SIXTEEN

TWENTY MINUTES LATER, Marc returned to the reception area shaking his head. "I'm really sorry."

"He wouldn't provide a sample?" Jay couldn't believe it. He'd been so certain that Marc would be able to convince his former coach that it was the honorable thing to do.

"Before he got sick, I have no doubt he would have cooperated. Coach Gifford taught us that we have to take responsibility for our actions—on the field and in real life, too."

"Sounds like he was a great coach."

"That's why I'm here," Marc answered simply. "But this disease has affected his mind. He's suspicious and paranoid about so many things. I couldn't risk upsetting him by forcing the issue."

"Did you mention Lillian Price?"

"Yeah. But I'm not sure it was a good idea. When he heard her name he started to cry." Marc handed the test kit back to Jay.

Damn. Jay had had such high hopes that this would turn out differently.

"Well, thanks for trying." Jay offered the younger man a business card. "If he changes his mind, will you call?"

"Sure," Marc said, but it was clear that he didn't believe there was much chance of that happening.

IT WAS TOO LATE in the day to take Oliver Crane's DNA sample to the lab, so Kate had to wait until the morning. She was so anxious, she arrived ten minutes before opening and stood stamping her feet in the cold until the front door was unlocked.

She'd been prepared to see Jay, waiting with a sample from Gary Gifford, but she was the only person in the lab as she handed over the test and filled out the paperwork.

Did that mean he hadn't had any more luck with Gifford than she had?

She hoped so. She was so close now, so very close.

She wanted to stay at the lab and wait for the results, but of course, that didn't make any sense. Still, she felt at a loss for what to do.

There was nothing more to be accomplished by going to the office. Until she'd been officially selected for the job, this was her only case.

She decided to go to an Internet café for breakfast. The café was one of those cozy, casual places, with a menu written on a blackboard in colored chalk, weathered wooden floors and tiny round tables matched with small, wooden chairs.

Kate bought a muffin and juice, then found a table next to the window. She ate slowly, gazing outside at the tail end of the morning rush. On the sidewalks she saw people with every shade of skin, dressed in clothing that ran the gamut from designer business wear to grungy casual.

Gray-haired executives brushed past multipierced and tattooed young adults. Beautifully coiffed women stepped around harried young parents with children in tow—on their way to schools or day cares, before heading into the office.

Kate's attention was drawn to the children, especially the babies and toddlers in strollers. They were the only ones, she thought, who were really looking and paying attention to the world around them.

Most of the adults had distracted expressions, as if mentally they were already at their place of employment. They were sipping from takeout coffee mugs, or talking into their cell phones.

It was the children who were taking in the world around them, wide-eyed and curious. Kate felt the familiar ache, the desperate need to be a mother.

In six more days, she would know for sure. According to her research, that was when she would be able to expect a reasonably accurate result from a home pregnancy test. But she wasn't holding out much hope. In fact, with each passing day she realized how foolish she'd been to even consider getting pregnant could be this easy.

Kate sighed, then logged in to the computer and hooked up to the Internet. One way or the other, either she or Jay were shortly going to be out of a job. It couldn't hurt to do some research. Find out what else was out there.

The most promising opportunity she found was with
the Ashenhurst Agency, located in SoHo. The firm was
quite a bit larger than The Fox & Fisher Detective
Agency, which would translate into less freedom and
more bureaucracy. But still, she jotted down the contact
information.

Then she called the office.

"Are you coming in today?" Nadine wanted to know.

"There isn't any point. I just dropped off Oliver
Crane's DNA sample."

"How exciting! Congratulations, Kate."

"They promised to rush the results to the agency.
When the envelope arrives, will you give me a call? I'll
probably be at home."

"Of course I will. Right away."

SEVERAL HOURS LATER, KATE was three chapters into a
crime novel, and still not captivated, when Jay called.

"I'm not sure what to do with myself," he said. "I've
typed up my final report and submitted my expenses."

"Waiting for the lab results is killing me," she admitted.

"Want to go for a walk?"

She hesitated. Was spending more time with Jay a
good idea? But she couldn't resist the opportunity to be
with him. "Sure." She grabbed her jacket and keys and
met him a few blocks from Riverside Park.

Though he was wearing his aviator sunglasses, she
could sense him watching her as she approached. She
stopped a few feet from him, awkwardly stuffing her
hands in her pockets.

"So. How are you?" she asked.

"Been better. I'm sorry I overreacted the other day. I want—" He cleared his throat. "It seems like it would be a good idea if we could be friends."

"I'd like that," she said.

They started walking again, and it seemed they'd only taken a few steps before they encountered a young mother with a side-by-side stroller.

"Twins?" Kate asked.

The mother nodded. She was probably asked this all the time, but she didn't seem to mind. "A boy and a girl. The only time I can get them to nap at the same time is when we go out for a walk."

"You're a baby magnet," Jay said once they were out of sight.

"Weren't they adorable? Did you see those dimples?"

Jay reached over, took her arm and tucked it under his own. Kate swallowed at this display of easy intimacy, but she didn't try to withdraw.

Because it felt good to be walking with Jay like this. It felt natural.

"We said when the competition was over, we'd share war stories," Jay reminded her.

"That's right, we did." And the contest between them *was* as good as over. Oliver Crane's results were going to give Hannah the answer she needed.

Kate glanced at Jay. "I wanted to know the worst thing that happened in all your years of flying planes."

"Still want to know?"

She nodded.

"Some pilots go a whole career without making an emergency landing. And some emergency landings are really just precautions. But on Christmas Eve two years ago, I was flying into LaGuardia when my left landing gear failed to lock into position."

Jay's face was white and Kate knew he was back there, in the cockpit on that night. She squeezed his hand to bring him to ground. "That sounds serious."

"It got my adrenaline racing," he agreed. "Part of the problem is, you never know for sure if the landing gear really is malfunctioning, or if there's just a glitch with the computer system. It was too dark for me to pass over the flight tower and have the air traffic controllers take a look for me. At any rate, even if the gears were down, they might not be locked. So I had to go into the landing blind."

It sounded terrifying to Kate. "How do you land a plane without wheels?"

"Well, I had the landing gear on the right side and the nose. But it's still a tricky thing, keeping the plane level to avoid the worst-case scenario."

"Which is…?"

"Landing off balance and cartwheeling the plane."

She covered her face at that appalling picture.

"Plenty of other stuff can go wrong, too. Fire. Crashing too hard on the runway…"

"Not good options."

"No. So, first we had to burn off surplus fuel, which meant circling the airport for about an hour. I had a full load that day—over two hundred lives including passengers and crew. A lot of them were saying their prayers, but my crew and I knew we had their safety in our hands."

"Talk about pressure."

"It's part of the job. Only you never know when your skills are going to be tested."

"Once you'd burned off the surplus fuel—what happened then?"

"I had to go in for the landing. The flight attendants did a great job of keeping the passengers from panicking as they braced for the worst."

"What about you? Were you scared?"

"No time for that. I had to stay one hundred percent focused on the landing. I touched down the right rear landing gear first. It held solid, so I held the nose up for as long as I could, but finally there was no more fighting gravity. I prayed that the landing gear on the nose would lock, and it did. The runway had been foamed down and I could see the emergency crews waiting to step in to help us. But I still had to get that left-hand side of the plane down to earth. That landing gear just wouldn't come down."

"How did you do it?"

"As gently as I could, but we still hit hard, with a god-awful noise. A few of the passengers started screaming, but they stopped once they realized we were safely on the ground. The underbelly of the plane was pretty beaten up, and we had some smoking, but no serious flames."

"You brought it down safely."

"Well, it was down, but not without damage. Most important, though, all the passengers and crew made a safe exit. There were only a few minor injuries from the rough landing."

"Weren't you tempted to hang up your wings after that?"

"Didn't even think about it. I was out the next morning, flying back to Frankfurt. Just another night's work, really."

"Don't be so humble. You were a hero, Jay. It's only thanks to you that all those people on that plane lived."

"Bringing them home safely is just part of the job. It must have been the same for you, Kate, working for the NYPD."

"You want my worst story now?"

He nodded.

"It doesn't have a happy ending."

He squeezed her hand.

"About three years ago I was called to the scene of a corner-store robbery. The thief shot the owner's daughter seconds before I arrived on the scene because she'd had trouble opening the safe. Her name was Biju and she was only sixteen years old."

"This world is some screwed-up place, isn't it?"

"I caught the guy, and EMS was on the scene in ten minutes. But they weren't fast enough to save the girl. Most likely, though, nothing could have saved her. Jay, she'd taken the bullet to her head. It was— it was awful."

He slipped an arm around her shoulder and pulled her close. "You caught the guy. Hopefully he paid for what he did."

"It's not much consolation when you consider a life was lost."

"God, Kate, over and over again you amaze me."

THE NEXT MORNING Jay received a call from Nadine. "I've just heard from BioFinds Lab," she said. "The DNA testing results are in. Can you be at the office in half an hour?"

"No problem." He walked to the subway stop with Eric, then they each headed in opposite directions. He'd given up accompanying his nephew to school. He'd decided that at this point he had to trust that Eric was going to classes. If he wasn't, Jay would probably find out at his next scheduled talk with the homeroom teacher or from a phone call from the police.

Nadine was waiting for him when he arrived. "Everyone's in the conference room."

"Including Kate?"

She nodded, then followed him down the hall, carrying a plate of bagels and cream cheese.

As Jay stepped into the room, he saw Kate standing alone by the window. She looked tired and tense, and her gaze went from his face to the envelope on the center of the table.

"All right," Lindsay said. "The big moment has arrived."

No one took a chair. It was as if all five of them were too nervous to sit.

"Kate?" Nathan picked up the envelope and handed it to her. "Why don't you do the honors."

Kate ran her tongue over her top lip, then tore the envelope open.

"Oh my God," Nadine said. "This is so exciting."

"These are the DNA test results for Oliver Crane," Kate reminded them unnecessarily. She glanced over the paper, then heaved a sigh. "Negative."

Silently, all five of them processed the news. Nadine was the first to speak.

"So…by the process of elimination, that means Gary Gifford is Hannah's father."

"That's right," Lindsay said. "Well done, Kate. You, too, Jay." She reached over to shake his hand. "I wish we could offer you both a job. I really do."

Nathan clasped his shoulder. "I'm sorry, buddy. But you gave it a great shot."

Jay nodded his thanks, his gaze still on Kate. She was taking her success modestly. In fact, she seemed a little uncomfortable with it.

He approached her, offering a hand. "Well done, Kate. You deserve the job."

"Nadine, could you please phone Hannah and tell her we'd like her to come to the office as soon as possible?" Lindsay asked. "This is the sort of news that ought to be delivered in person."

"I agree," Jay said. "It's going to be a bit of a shock. Nadine, you should tell her to bring her husband along if at all possible."

"What do you mean by 'a bit of a shock'?" Lindsay asked. "Is there something we don't know about?"

Jay waited, looking at Kate to fill in the blanks. When

he realized she was as confused as the others, he asked, "Didn't you find out why Gifford was in the care home?"

"I asked, but they wouldn't tell me." Her eyes narrowed. "But you know, don't you? How did you find out? I assumed he wouldn't talk to you, either."

"He wouldn't. But I talked to the music teacher at Brooklyn Heights High School."

"The woman he loved?" she asked softly.

He nodded. "She told me why he took early retirement. Coach Gifford has Huntington's disease."

"Oh, no," Nadine said. "Poor Hannah." As everyone in the room turned in her direction, she explained, "I have a cousin who married into a family with that disease. The offspring have a fifty-fifty chance of being a carrier."

"And if that happens, they are sure to contract the disease themselves, and have a fifty-fifty chance of passing it on to their children," Jay added.

"Oh my God," Lindsay said. Everyone fell silent.

"The good news," Nadine said quietly after the shock had worn off, "is that Hannah can get tested."

"I'm not so sure she and her husband will consider that good news," Nathan said drily. "But I don't see any way around this. She hired us for information, and we found it. Now it's our duty to share it with her."

HANNAH AND JEREMY managed to make it to the agency on their lunch break. Both arrived breathless, and hopeful, holding hands as they entered the conference room together.

Jay couldn't stand to look them in the eyes, so he got up to pour water for everyone. The bagels at the center of the table hadn't been touched, and Lindsay offered them to their clients. Unaware that soon they would have no appetite for food, they each helped themselves.

"We'll get started as soon as Kate—" Lindsay stopped talking as Kate breezed in, bringing the chill from the city streets with her.

She'd said she was going for a walk, yet her skin was pale. Maybe she was just upset about the upcoming meeting. She kept her gaze on her notebook, which was okay, since Jay wouldn't have been able to meet her eyes, anyway. He didn't begrudge that she'd won the competition. But he realized that this would probably be the last time they saw one another. He wasn't as happy about that as he ought to be.

"Hi, everyone. I hope I didn't keep you waiting." Kate settled into a chair opposite from Jay, folded her hands on the table, then looked expectantly toward Lindsay.

"We were just starting," Lindsay assured her.

Despite Kate's apparent ease, Jay could tell she was stressed. As a cop she must have had plenty of experience telling people bad news, but this was a matter close to her heart. Kate, more than anyone at this table, knew what it was like to want a child of her own.

"You've found my father?" Clearly the mood in the room, which was cautious and restrained, had Hannah puzzled. She checked out everyone's faces, then turned to Jeremy for reassurance.

"Yes, we have," Nathan finally said. "Hannah's father

is Gary Gifford. Jay and Kate both found him in a nursing home in Brooklyn Heights—"

"A nursing home?" Jeremy asked. "He can't be that old."

Nathan held up a hand, asking for a moment to explain. "Kate determined that Gary was Hannah's father by the process of elimination, since he refused to provide a sample of his DNA. We have test results from Oliver Crane, and we already had results from James Morgan, so I'm afraid there can be no doubt."

"What do you mean, you're *afraid?*"

Kate bravely took the floor. She leaned toward Hannah, her own eyes glistening with tears. "The reason your birth father was in a care home at such an early age is because he suffers from a genetic neurological disorder."

"Did you say *genetic?*" Jeremy asked sharply.

Kate nodded. "I'm afraid Gary Gifford suffers from Huntington's disease."

"Huntington's? Are you sure?" Jeremy spoke in a loud voice. He let go of his wife's hand.

"I'm afraid so," Kate replied, her tone a quiet, calm contrast to Jeremy's.

There was momentary silence as the couple absorbed the devastating news.

"I worked in a nursing home one summer," Jeremy said. "I saw people with that affliction. Oh my God." He buried his face in his hands.

Hannah looked very small and alone now, with her husband falling apart on one side of her, and the information slowly percolating into her consciousness. "Huntington's is fatal, isn't it?"

"It's a neurological disease that affects a person's emotions, intellect and ability to move. The symptoms usually present during middle age, and yes, after a period of ten years or so, it is eventually fatal."

"Oh, God." Hannah placed a shaking hand over her mouth.

Kate reached over to touch her shoulder. "You aren't automatically a carrier, Hannah."

"What are my chances of—?" She couldn't manage to finish the sentence, just looked mutely at Kate.

Kate closed her eyes briefly before saying, "Fifty percent."

"Oh, no." Hannah's face crumpled like a child's and Jay wished her husband would console her, but Jeremy still seemed in a state of shock.

With a deep breath, Hannah held her tears at bay. "So I could get this disease *and* I could pass it on to my kids?"

"*If* you are a carrier," Kate pointed out. "If you aren't, then there is no risk to having children."

An eerie, calm acceptance seemed to settle over Hannah. "You know, Jeremy, I thought you were being paranoid when you insisted that we find my biological father before having kids. Now I see how right you were. And I wouldn't blame you if you didn't want to be married to me anymore."

Jeremy stared at her, horrified.

Jay was pretty shocked, too. If that husband didn't hug her soon, then he was going to go over there and do it. But before either he or Jeremy could move, Hannah rushed out of the room. A second later they heard the reception door slam shut.

"Is this a case where it might have been better to let sleeping dogs lie?" Nadine asked half an hour later. Her eyes were pink and puffy as she poured from a fresh pot of coffee.

Kate held out her mug, needing the shot of caffeine in the absence of anything stronger. No one had left the conference room since Jeremy ran out after his wife.

"I can't believe what a jerk her husband was." Jay was still fuming.

"Give him a break," Lindsay said. "He had a big shock, too. And would they be better off not knowing about Hannah's family's medical history? I don't think so. Can't they do prescreening on the embryo, to make sure the child won't be a carrier?"

"Yes," Kate agreed, wishing it were just that simple. She'd been stewing over the situation since she'd found out why Gifford was in the nursing home. "But if the test comes back positive for Huntington's, then Hannah will know, for certain, that she's a carrier, too. Would you rather live the rest of your life dreading the eventual onset of Huntington's, or be blissfully ignorant of the risk?"

"I wouldn't want to know," Nadine said firmly.

"I think I would," Lindsay said.

Kate glanced at the guys. Both of them shrugged.

"It puts Hannah in a tough position, for sure," Jay said.

"Unfortunately we can't do anything to help her,"

Nathan said. "But we have our own difficult situation to deal with here."

Lindsay went to stand by him, her expression serious. "Nathan and I are both very impressed with your work, Jay. Given that you're the one who learned about the Huntington's…well, that makes it all the more difficult not to offer you a position here."

"I understand," he said. "I've already packed up my stuff. There wasn't that much." He nodded at Kate. "The office is all yours."

Jay headed for the door.

But Kate stepped in front of him.

"Wait, Jay. When I left the office right now, I didn't just go for a walk. I made a phone call."

Where was she headed with this? He studied her eyes. She was clearly upset, but he didn't understand why.

"I've been offered another job," she explained. "It's with a large agency in SoHo. I was just speaking to the managing partner, Everett Ashenhurst. When he heard I had ten years experience with the NYPD, he offered me a position on the spot."

"But why, Kate?" Lindsay burst out. "This job is yours. You found Hannah's father. You won the contest, fair and square."

"But Jay found out about the Huntington's. In a way, that was even more important than identifying the man. He deserves the job."

"That's not right," he said. "You earned the job, Kate. Not me."

"The money is excellent at the Ashenhurst Agency

and so is the benefit package," she told him. "Besides, I've already accepted the new position. It's a done deal."

Jay just stood there, shaking his head. She could see how conflicted he felt, but she knew she was doing the right thing.

Even more important, she finally understood *why*.

Why she'd wanted to have a baby with this man.

Why she didn't have the heart to take this position, even though it was her dream job.

The answer was simple. She was in love with Jay.

CHAPTER SEVENTEEN

IF IT HADN'T BEEN FOR ERIC, there was no way Jay would have let Kate walk out of the Fox & Fisher offices. As it was, Nathan had to talk him into staying. Even Lindsay, who he'd thought didn't even like him, told him he'd be a fool to walk away.

"When Kate makes up her mind, she never changes it."

Jay recognized this truth about Kate, and reluctantly he let Nadine walk him through the stacks of paperwork that were necessary to get him on the company payroll.

He had to admit that it was a big relief to have a regular paycheck again. And the flexible hours at Fox & Fisher meshed nicely with Eric's timetable.

Still, the job was not as much fun without Kate.

Even Eric noticed her absence from their lives.

"What happened to that redheaded cop?" he asked one night over spaghetti and meatballs. "Are you still working together?"

"Not anymore."

"But you're friends, right? Maybe she could come over some time."

"I don't think so. Her new job is keeping her pretty busy." No ties, she promised him, after they'd had sex. But he hadn't counted on wanting ties.

It seemed the sex hadn't worked. At least he'd heard nothing from Lindsay or Nadine about Kate being pregnant. That was the sort of news he figured would get around.

So she wasn't pregnant. And he was relieved. But not as relieved as he'd expected to be.

TWO WEEKS INTO her new job, Kate was beginning to think the Twentieth Precinct hadn't been so bad after all. The last thing she'd expected when she'd switched to private practice was to be bored out of her skull.

She should have looked over the case files before she'd accepted this job. Ashenhurst Agency specialized in high-level corporate accounts, and while the jobs were lucrative, the work was largely done over the Internet and phone, from the comfort of the office, and they all involved massive quantities of reports and paperwork.

Kate missed being out in the field. She missed dealing with clients face-to-face and knowing that she was making a difference in someone's life.

Even worse, the people she worked with were older and duller. They ate their lunches at their desks and disappeared out the door promptly at six. Maybe she wasn't being fair to them, maybe she'd develop some friendships over time, but so far it wasn't looking good.

The regular hours would be great if she had a life of

her own, but she was still living alone and hating it. She really had to get serious about adopting a kitten.

Face it, she told herself. *You miss Lindsay and Nathan and Nadine.*

And then there was Jay.

He'd told her she deserved the whole package, something he couldn't give her. She loved children and she still wanted to have children.

But she was beginning to think she wanted Jay more.

From the cubicle next to hers came the sound of a sandwich being unwrapped, then the unmistakable odor of tuna fish.

Lunchtime already. *My, how time flies.* Kate closed down her computer then got up from her chair. She didn't feel like eating, but she did need a little fresh air and sunshine.

Outside, she found herself heading for a nearby drugstore. She went up and down the aisles, stocking up on a few of the essentials.

And then she came to the pregnancy tests.

She studied the rows of boxes. She was still certain that she wasn't pregnant. But…she hadn't had her period. True, she was only one day late. It would probably start tomorrow and this would be a total waste of money….

She bought a kit anyway.

She stuffed the box into her leather bag after she'd paid for it. Back at the office, she went to the washroom. Moving slowly, because she knew there was zero chance the result was going to be positive, she opened the cardboard box, removed the contents and read the directions.

Simple. All she needed to do was pee. So she did that. Then she sat and waited and waited.

Slowly a word appeared in the little window.

The word was *pregnant*.

She couldn't breathe. She wanted to cry. She wanted to laugh.

It had happened. She was going to have a baby.

KATE CALLED LINDSAY and asked her to meet her at the Stool Pigeon after work.

"I have news. And it's big," she told her friend the second she saw her.

"Wait a minute. Don't I at least get to order a drink first?" Lindsay settled onto the bench seat opposite Kate.

"No. I'm pregnant."

"What?" Lindsay dropped the menu onto the floor. "You are kidding me."

"I'm going to have a baby."

"The generally accepted definition for pregnant. Yes, I get that part, but good Lord, how did it happen? You didn't go to a sperm bank?" She searched Kate's face for the answer and when she couldn't see one, tried again. "Was it an immaculate conception? Or did you meet a new guy? Don't tell me you got back together with Conner?"

"No, no, and no chance in hell." Kate put her hands on either side of her face, not sure if she was going to actually tell Lindsay the truth. But she had to tell Lindsay. She would burst if she couldn't tell somebody.

And then, out of the blue, Lindsay guessed. "It's Jay, isn't it? He's the father."

Kate nodded.

"I knew something was going on with the two of you. That day in the conference room when we had the first update with Hannah, you two looked guilty as sin."

"What can I say? You have good instincts." She wondered what Lindsay would say if she told her *where* it had happened. But that was private between her and Jay. Not everything had to be shared.

Lindsay grinned. "This is so exciting. I'm so happy for you guys. Where is Jay? I never would have guessed anything this good was happening based on the way he's been acting in the office lately."

"Why? How has he been acting?"

"Almost depressed, I'd say. But maybe he's just overwhelmed about becoming a father."

"But he isn't. We had a deal. He did this for me. He doesn't want children. Ever. He's even considered having a vasectomy. He feels that strongly about it."

"Hang on. I'm not sure I'm following. Are you and Jay a couple or not?"

"Not."

"Oh." Lindsay's smile faded a little. "But this is still good news…right?"

"The best. It's exactly what I wanted. I couldn't be happier."

"Well, then I'm happy for you, too." Lindsay leaned forward. "Does Jay know yet?"

"I wasn't going to tell him. That was the deal."

"He isn't getting involved with the child—that's fine, I suppose, if it's what you both want. But, Kate, you *have* to tell him."

ON SATURDAY ERIC SAID he was going out with friends and would be back for dinner. Jay couldn't think of any reason to say no. All week long Eric was busy with school, tutoring and basketball. He had to be allowed some free time.

Still, Jay wished he knew these friends of his.

"What are you planning to do?"

"I don't know. Just hang out. Maybe shoot some baskets." He pulled his hat over his hair.

"Want to invite your buddies over for pizza tonight?"

"Not really."

He could hear in Eric's voice that he thought it was a lame idea. Well, maybe it was. Jay could remember being fourteen. That was part of the problem here. There was just too much trouble for a kid to get into. Especially a kid who'd had very little guidance in his life.

Short of locking Eric in his room for the rest of his school years, though, there wasn't much he could do.

Once Eric had gone, the apartment felt eerily quiet. It was hard for Jay to remember that for years and years it had always been that way.

He straightened out a few things around the apartment, then picked up the phone. Nathan had suggested they might go to the gym this weekend. But before he could dial his number, the phone rang in his hand.

"Ready for a workout?" he asked.

"Pardon me?"

Hell, it was Kate. "Sorry. I thought you were Nathan."

"Instead of a workout, would you be interested in a walk?"

With Kate? Definitely. "Same place as last time?"

"Sure. I'm leaving right now. I'll meet you there."

He pulled on running shoes, grabbed his keys and wallet, and was out the door sixty seconds later. Despite that, she arrived before he did. He caught up to her as she was ordering hot dogs from a street vendor.

"Ketchup or mustard?" she asked.

He'd never seen her with her hair in a ponytail before. She had cute ears. And freckles on the back of her neck. He hadn't noticed *those* before.

"Ketchup or mustard?" she repeated.

"Both."

Kate was wearing a powder-blue sweater that made her skin glow. He was glad that despite the sun, she wasn't wearing sunglasses. He liked being able to see her eyes.

Once they had their hot dogs, they walked in silence for a while, enjoying the food and the sun on their backs.

When he'd swallowed the last bite, Jay sighed. The day hadn't started out that well, but it had definitely taken a turn for the better. "The office isn't the same without you. How are you liking the new job?"

"It's fine."

"Just fine?"

"The pay is excellent."

"But do you like the work? Do you like the people?"

"Also, my new firm has excellent benefits."

"Okay, but—"

"Including a very good health plan."

He paused, realizing she was trying to tell him something. "A good health plan, huh?"

"Yes. It'll come in handy in about, oh, eight months from now."

"Kate?" He grabbed her shoulders and stared deeply into her eyes. "Are you serious?"

She nodded. "It happened, Jay. I'm going to have a baby."

His gaze slid down to her belly, which was as flat as ever. Oh my God. Just the one time they'd been together, but that had been enough. He felt overwhelmed with emotions he couldn't even name.

"Don't get the wrong idea. I'm not going back on our deal. I'm just telling you because I thought you had a right to know. Well, Lindsay thought you had a right to know. And after all we went through with Hannah, I had to agree with her."

He was too overcome to speak.

"You're not upset are, you? Maybe I shouldn't have—"

"I'm glad you told me, Kate. I'm just—surprised. I assumed as the weeks went by that you didn't get pregnant."

"I assumed the same thing. I thought, what are the odds, right? And I didn't feel any different. I kept hoping that I would, but I didn't."

"You look the same."

"I know." She smiled at him, her eyes shining with

incredulous wonder. "This is such a major thing. You'd think there'd be *something* on the outside to match what's happening on the inside."

He squeezed her shoulders. "There is one thing. You're glowing, Kate. Absolutely glowing."

Her chin quivered and instinctively he wrapped his arms around her. The smell of her hair was deliciously familiar. It was a scent that could stop him cold if he happened to catch a hint of it among a crowd of strangers.

When he released her from the hug, she wiped a tear from her eye. "Thank you so much, Jay."

"You're sure you're going to be okay? The crying…is it happy crying?" Maybe faced with the reality of pregnancy, she'd started to regret her decision to be a single parent. Some ideas were better in theory than they turned out to be in practice.

"Absolutely, Jay. Please don't worry about a thing. I promise I'll do well by our baby."

Despite the fact that tears were still welling in her eyes, he believed her. He was glad she still thought they'd done the right thing. But his own emotions were a lot more complicated. He couldn't come close to sorting them out.

For one thing, why did he wish that she wasn't quite so self-sufficient about the whole thing?

TELLING JAY THAT SHE WAS expecting had been the right thing to do. The fact that she couldn't make herself stop crying was just a sign that hormones were coursing through her body.

Perfectly natural.

Probably lots of women went through this.

Jay insisted on walking her home and when they reached her apartment, he asked if he could come in for a bit until he was certain she was all right.

In other words, until she had managed to calm down.

Jay made her tea, then sat beside her on the sofa. He was being so sweet. She thought this might be easier if he wasn't.

She grabbed the last tissue from a box that Jay had placed beside her. She wiped the corners of her eyes, then blew her nose and tossed the used tissue into an overflowing waste can.

"This is just hormones," she said for about the twentieth time.

"You were wanting some outward sign that you were different. Maybe this is it." The shock that had glazed over Jay's eyes when she'd told him the news was beginning to fade.

"Any idea when the baby is due?" he asked.

She nodded. "December fifteenth. I found this cool calculator online. All I had to do was type in the date of my last period."

"December seems like a long way away."

"I know." She hugged one of the sofa cushions to her chest. "The program works the other way, too. You can type in your birthday and find out when you were conceived. It turns out I was conceived on December twenty-fifth."

He grinned. "Under the Christmas tree, probably."

"I wonder if my parents knew that's when it happened. I doubt they would have appreciated the irony if they had." She knew they hadn't considered her arrival any sort of gift.

She put down the cushion, then had some more tea. "You know, I can't stop thinking about Hannah and Jeremy."

"Because you're having a baby and that's what they wanted?"

"Yes. It just seems so cruel that out of three potential fathers, the one who had turned out to be Hannah's biological dad had to be the only one who wasn't healthy."

"I wish we'd been able to get a sample from Gifford," Jay said. "Just to be one hundred percent sure we had the right guy."

"But who else could it be? We checked with Rebecca. She only gave us the three men." Kate's face tingled as a wild idea occurred to her. "Do you remember Hannah's birth date?"

"I'm sure it's in the file, but I don't recall offhand."

Kate was suddenly too excited to sit still. "I just had an idea. It's a long shot, but I'd like to check it out. Do you have time to run to the office right now?"

Jay checked his watch. "I've got a couple hours until Eric is supposed to be home. But why—" He stopped himself as he figured out what she was after. "You want to calculate the date that Hannah was conceived?"

"Yes." Kate was already putting on a sweater and slipping into her shoes. "Do you have the office keys on you?"

He patted the pocket of his jeans. "Yes."

"JULY FIRST," JAY SAID, reading from the file as Kate logged on to his computer. He hadn't changed the password since she'd worked here, so she had no trouble getting in.

"Let me see if I can find that Web site." Kate's fingers flew over the keyboard as she tried various words in the search engine. "Good. Here it is."

He went to stand behind her, watching as she filled out the birth date then clicked on the calculate button. The date that appeared on the screen, the date when Hannah was conceived, was October fifth.

"Good Lord," he said, trying to process what this meant. "I can't think of any university where frosh week lasts that long."

Kate clasped her hands together and looked up at him. "This is so wonderful, Jay. You know what it means?"

"Gary Gifford can't be her father."

"Right. Rebecca's husband, John, is her father. Let's call the Trotters right now and see if he'll provide a DNA sample. With any luck we'll have good news for Hannah and her husband by Wednesday at the latest."

CHAPTER EIGHTEEN

ON WEDNESDAY KATE TOLD Everett Ashenhurst that she needed to take a long lunch hour in order to clear up a case from her old job. She took a taxi to the Upper West Side and arrived at the offices at the same time as Hannah and Jeremy.

The young couple seemed apprehensive as they made their way up the stairs.

Kate felt nostalgic as she greeted Nadine, then followed the Youngs into the boardroom. Lindsay, Nathan and Jay were all waiting for them. Jay tried to catch her eye, but she just smiled vaguely and found herself a seat.

She was afraid she would give herself away by looking at Jay too often, smiling too openly. She needed to guard her emotions every second of this meeting, which wouldn't be easy.

After pleasantries were exchanged, Lindsay asked Jay if he wanted to take charge of the meeting.

He looked at Kate. In truth, she knew he'd hardly stopped looking at her since she'd entered the room. "Kate figured this out. She should be the one to tell them."

She acknowledged his graciousness with a slight nod

of her head. Then she turned to Hannah and Jeremy. They were sitting beside one another, holding hands.

"Hannah, do you remember that we determined Gary Gifford was your biological father by the process of elimination?"

The young woman nodded. "You had DNA samples from James Morgan and Oliver Crane. Both came out negative, so that meant the third man—Gary Gifford— was my dad."

"We reasoned there was no other possibility because your birth mother told us that she had only been with three men. And that was true, in the month of September."

Hannah and Jeremy exchanged uncertain glances. Kate could see that they were anxious and she wanted to give them the good news as soon as possible. But she had to explain this properly.

"Hannah, when Jay and I spoke to your birth mother, she told us something else. She said that she'd started to date the man she eventually married about a month after she got pregnant. In her mind, she got pregnant during frosh week, which was the beginning of September."

"Yes. She told me all that, too," Hannah agreed.

"But you were born on July first. The average gestation period from conception to birth is two hundred and sixty-six days. I've checked the numbers several times. There is no way you could have been conceived in early September."

Hannah and Jeremy both looked shocked by this.

"What are you saying?" Jeremy asked, perching on the edge of his chair.

"I'm saying that Hannah's birth father is John Trotter. We had DNA tests done to be certain and this time there is absolutely no doubt."

"Oh my God." Hannah brought her hands slowly to her face. "Really? You're sure?"

"Your mom used protection every time she was with John Trotter. That's why she never considered he could be the dad."

"You're saying the protection failed?" Jeremy's face reddened and tears came to his eyes. He reached an arm out to his wife and pulled her to him.

"We have the DNA test right here if you want to see it," Jay said.

Jeremy did. He checked the file. "Thank God."

"So…I won't get Huntington's? And we can have a baby?" Hannah was still taking it all in.

Kate could hardly see anymore, because her eyes were flooded with tears. Lindsay passed a box of tissues around the room. Even Jay and Nathan needed one.

"I—I'm shaking," Hannah said as her husband tried to draw her to her feet. "I—I still can't believe this."

Through her tears, Kate grinned. Unable to stop herself, she glanced across the room at Jay. He winked back at her. Talk about job satisfaction. It didn't get better than this.

THERE WAS A TOY STORE a few blocks from the office and on Monday evening Jay found himself staring in the front window. He could see a display of stuffed animals. One of them reminded him of a small white bear his sister had had when she was very young. She'd slept with it every night and because she carried it with her wherever she went during the day, it had been inevitable that she would lose it.

She'd cried every night for several weeks after it was gone. He'd been six at the time and she was four. He didn't have access to much money, but he collected bottles from the street and pulled them out of trash cans until he had enough to buy her a new stuffed bear.

But she had never loved it as much as the first one.

Jay felt as if something very heavy was pressing on his chest. He'd been feeling this way ever since Tracy died, but it was getting worse, not better, with time.

Especially since Kate had told him her news.

He knew his role in her life was finished now.

But he couldn't stop thinking about her. Wondering how she was feeling and if she was still crying at the slightest provocation.

Though she kept blaming hormonal surges, he wondered if maybe she wasn't quite as strong as she thought she was.

He went inside the store and picked up the little white bear. "Would you put this in a gift bag, please?" he asked the cashier as he pulled out his wallet.

TUESDAY, AT NOON, Jay happened to have some business in the SoHo neighborhood—okay, he'd manufactured a good excuse to be in the area. He figured he'd drop in on Kate and see if she was free for lunch.

The Ashenhurst Agency was bigger than he expected, occupying a large loft building on Broadway. Inside, the ambience was utilitarian. The open space was divided into pods of workstations, four cubicles per pod.

He approached the receptionist and asked for Kate Cooper. Less than a minute later she was walking toward him. He'd never found her anything but beautiful, but he was struck at how pale and tired she seemed.

"Can you get away for lunch?" he asked.

"Love to."

Outside, her color brightened and she seemed like the old Kate again. As they walked along the street, he asked how she was feeling and whether she'd seen a doctor yet.

"I have an appointment with my OB next Monday."

They chose a café and sat at a table for two near the back.

"That place—the Ashenhurst Agency—doesn't seem like you. I don't see how you can be happy there. I feel so guilty—"

"Stop, Jay. Don't. I told you it's the perfect situation for me right now." Her fingertips tapped on the wooden table as they waited for a server.

She seemed uptight. Maybe this would be a good time to distract her. Jay pulled the gift bag out from his briefcase and placed it in front of her.

She tilted her head, and her silky hair fell to one shoulder. "What's this for?"

Suddenly, he felt silly. "I saw it in a store window and I couldn't resist."

She peeked in the box, then compressed her lips. As she pulled out the little bear, her chin started to wobble.

"Oh, no. I made you cry."

"It doesn't take much these days." She stroked the soft fur. "He's so adorable. Thank you, Jay. But you didn't have to do this. I hope you know that."

"I thought—" he started, and then he stopped. What *had* he been thinking? That their child should have some sort of token gift from the father who didn't want any part of his life?

And in a flash it hit him. He *did* want to be a part of this baby's life. And even more important, he wanted to be a part of Kate's.

Because he loved her. He was crazy about her.

He touched her hand. "Kate—"

"It's okay, Jay," she said. "I should have known you'd have trouble walking away from the responsibility of having fathered a child. Now you feel trapped and it's all my fault. I shouldn't have listened to Lindsay. I shouldn't have told you about the baby."

"No." That wasn't what he meant at all. But Kate had already made up her mind about his motives.

Gently she placed the bear back into the bag. "I'm sure the baby will love this. But I don't want you to buy any more gifts. We had a deal and it was meant to protect us both. I wanted a baby and you didn't."

Jay dropped his eyes and shifted anxiously in his chair.

"You're used to being the responsible one and taking care of people," she continued. "But this time you don't have to be that guy. I'm more than capable of raising this child on my own."

"I never doubted that." But what if he *wanted* to fill the roles of husband and father?

Yeah, right. What was he thinking? Had he forgotten who he was and where he came from? He'd only mess things up for Kate and the baby if he tried to be a part of their lives.

"But I still feel like you've had a raw deal. I shouldn't have taken the job at Fox & Fisher."

"Yes, you should have. For as long as Eric's living with you, you need that job. Everything is fine just the way it is."

He glanced up long enough to see that her eyes were shimmering with tears again. He didn't think she was right. She wasn't fine and neither was he.

But maybe this was just as good as things were going to get for either of them.

ON FRIDAY ERIC BROUGHT an envelope home from school. "It's my report card," he said on his way to the fridge. "You have to sign it."

Jay didn't want to look. Lately he and Eric had achieved a state of truce where Eric followed most of the rules Jay laid out without complaining and Jay tried not to play the heavy any more than he had to.

Still, he lived in fear of getting another phone call from the cops. This time maybe for something more dangerous than skipping classes—though that would be bad enough.

Jay picked up the envelope as Eric brushed by with an apple and a hunk of cheddar cheese in his hands. A second later, he heard the TV go on.

Maybe he should sit down.

He opened the envelope and removed a sheet of paper. He scanned down the column for the third-term results and frowned. Was he reading correctly? They were all A's.

He checked the first-term column and the second term, too. Again, all A's.

In the section for comments, Eric's homeroom teacher had written, "After the death of his mother, Eric had a few weeks where his attendance was spotty and he had difficulty concentrating. But he quickly recovered and managed to pull up his marks to his usual excellent standard."

Jay sat there for a long time, adjusting his perceptions of his nephew. Then he took a pen and signed on the designated line.

Tracy's signature was there, as well, for the previous term results. His chest ached at the sight of her familiar, left-slanting script.

He put the report card back into the envelope for safekeeping, then joined Eric in the living room. His nephew was watching an episode of *Supernatural*. Jay settled in to watch it with him, and when it was over, he turned off the set.

Immediately Eric got up to leave.

"Hang on a minute. Eric—I owe you an apology."

His nephew looked at him, his expression cautious.

"That's an amazing report card you brought home. You should be very proud of yourself."

"What did you expect? That I was failing?"

"I assumed that because you'd missed so many classes your marks would be poor."

"You always think the worst of me. When I skip classes you think it's because I'm into drugs or committing crimes or something."

"Well…what *do* you do when you cut out of school?"

"I go for walks. I ride the subway. I think."

Jay pictured his nephew, alone for hours, and his heart ached. He had been processing his mother's death, in his own way, and Jay wished that he had shown more respect for that.

"I'm not going to do anything stupid," Eric continued. "You can't get into the police academy if you have a record."

Eric wanted to be a cop? Suddenly Jay remembered a younger Eric talking about just that. At the time Jay had figured he would change his mind a dozen times before he grew up. But he obviously hadn't.

"So that's why you were asking Kate Cooper all those questions about the police academy."

"Well, yeah. Why else would I be interested in her? She's way too old for me."

Jay laughed. "God, Eric. I've been such an idiot."

But this was one case where he didn't mind being wrong. His nephew was smart, focused and definitely on the right track. He was just so bloody thankful.

He went over and gave his nephew a good, strong hug. "Way to go, Eric. You're one amazing kid."

Eric pulled out from the hug, smiling. "Does this mean I don't have a curfew anymore?"

"Dream on, buddy." Jay brushed his hand over Eric's blond curls. "When you turn sixteen we'll talk."

JAY DIDN'T REALIZE how much he'd been weighted down with worry about Eric until he discovered his concerns were unfounded. Not that Eric was perfect, or that there wouldn't be challenges down the road.

But hell. Eric was an A student. More important, he had a goal for his life. Jay knew from experience that having something to work toward could make all the difference. His own aspirations to become a pilot had provided the motivation for him to finish school and go on to college.

Hopefully Eric's desire to be a cop would do the same for him.

On Sunday night Jay slept deeply. He dreamed he was in the captain's seat of his much-loved 777. Visibility was unlimited. The sky was robin's egg–blue above, fading to aquamarine at the horizon. His hands on the controls were steady. He was in his zone.

He turned to share the moment with his copilot, but Kate was seated next to him. "Uh…I didn't know you had your pilot's license."

She gave him her trademark cocky smile. "You don't know everything about me, Jay Savage."

He woke up sweating and couldn't get back to sleep.

Monday morning, he called Lindsay at home. "Do you know the name of Kate's OB?"

"Sure, it's Dr. Janssen. Meg got the referral for her."

"Do you know the address?"

"I could find out. But, Jay—I thought your role in all this was finished?"

"You think I'm the kind of guy who gets a woman pregnant then walks away?"

"No. I mean, *yes*. Kate told me that was the deal. Was she wrong?"

"We discussed something like that," he admitted. He couldn't stand still. His mind was two steps ahead of him, planning what needed to be done. "But it's not working for me."

"Oh, boy. I warned Kate this could get complicated."

"Actually, from where I stand, it couldn't be more simple."

JAY PHONED THE OB NEXT. "This is Jay Savage. I'm the father of Kate Cooper's baby. Could you please remind me what time our appointment is?"

"Ten-thirty this morning, Mr. Savage."

"Thank you very much."

KATE'S OBSTETRICIAN'S OFFICE was three subway stops from his apartment. Jay clambered into the first available car then grabbed on to a metal pole. As the train jerked forward, he surrendered his body to the swaying motion. Over the past few weeks, he'd grown accustomed to the rhythm. Now, like Eric, he could let go of the metal bars before the train screeched to a stop, and zip out of the doors ahead of the crowd. But he didn't think he'd ever truly get used to traveling underground.

Shoulder to shoulder with other commuters, he made his way along the platform, up the stairs, then out to a blue-sky morning. He checked street signs and address numbers, finally locating the medical office building he was searching for.

Only a few steps away, he stopped.

There was Kate, her red hair and cream-colored coat standing out in the dreary landscape. He felt the kind of rush he normally experienced with liftoff, in that instant when the plane defied gravity and rose above the tarmac. It was a feeling of being completely alive and completely present in a moment of time. He was so overcome, he actually stopped walking, frozen in wonderment.

And then she saw him.

Her first reaction was to smile, but a frown was right on its heels. "Jay? What on earth are you doing here?"

"It isn't a coincidence." He came up beside her and took her hand. "Maybe it isn't gentlemanly of me, but I'm reneging on our agreement."

"But—"

"I don't want to be out of the picture where our baby is concerned. I'm happy to let you run the show—this isn't about me questioning your ability to be a wonderful mother."

"I hope not."

"One day this kid inside you is going to want to know who his daddy is. It's only natural, Kate. And I don't want him to have to hire a private investigator in order to find out."

"Oh, Jay." She covered her mouth with her free hand and stared at him.

"Is it all right if I come to this appointment with you?"

Her smile was sad, but accepting. "If you're sure it's what you need to do."

KATE WAS SHOCKED that Jay had shown up for her appointment. She'd tried so hard to make it clear that he was under absolutely no obligation where her pregnancy was concerned. Yet it had to be obligation that had brought him here. He'd pretty much admitted as much when he'd said their child had a right to know its father.

He tucked his hand under her elbow and walked with her the rest of the way. His strong presence by her side was a comfort, but she knew his being there had nothing to do with her, and everything to do with the baby inside her.

In the waiting room, they went up together to talk to the receptionist. Kate was given some forms to fill out, and he sat with her, reading over her shoulder.

There were two other fathers in the waiting room. Both were wearing wedding rings.

She looked away. Once Jay had told her she deserved the whole package. A man who loved her, children, pets, whatever she wanted. And she'd thought she could have all that, too, only not in the traditional order. Now she knew that dream was impossible. Because the man she loved would only see her as a responsibility.

She was asked to pee in a cup, then she and Jay were taken to a room where she was weighed and her blood pressure was taken.

All the while, she was fighting to find emotional equilibrium, torn between the urge to cry and a competing urge to rail out in anger.

When they were finally alone in the room, her sitting on the examining bed, him restlessly prowling, she was able to speak freely. "Just how involved are you planning to be?"

"I guess that's up to us to figure out."

"So I do get some say in this?" She folded her hands on her lap. She was unaccustomed to feeling vulnerable, but that was exactly how she did feel.

"I'm sorry if I upset you by coming here." Jay paced restlessly from one side of the room to the other, clearly a foreign element in this space. "I thought you might like some support."

He was always trying to do the right thing for other people. That was one of the qualities she found so exceptional in him. "I appreciate the thought. But maybe you could have called me ahead of time instead of showing up out of the blue."

He stopped in front of her and picked up her hands. His touch was tender. For that matter, so was his expression.

God help her, she was starting to cry again. Kate didn't bother trying to fight it this time.

"Kate, sweetheart. Do you want me to leave?"

She had no idea how to answer him. Because what she wanted was impossible. She wanted him to be here. But out of love. Not just for the baby, but for her, too.

A knock sounded on the door, and Dr. Janssen strolled in, a sensible-looking woman with grayish-blond hair, a stethoscope around her neck and Kate's brand-new file in her hands.

"Congratulations, Kate and Jay. I'm happy to confirm that you are indeed going to have a baby. Now let's have a good look at Mom and make sure everything is off to the best start possible."

"Do you have to go back to work now?" Jay asked.

The appointment was over and they were back on the street. Kate didn't bother buttoning her jacket. The air was much warmer now. And she could see buds on the trees. Spring was finally here.

"I should," she said. "But I'm not going to." She couldn't imagine heading back into her boring little cubicle to do her boring research job, after everything that had happened today.

She wanted to be over-the-moon excited about the baby—and a part of her was. But she had so many other feelings to process right now.

She longed for the simple anger she had felt when she'd found out Conner had been cheating on her. In the end she'd recovered from that heartbreak with amazing ease.

It would be different with Jay.

"Let's walk," he suggested.

She didn't have a better plan for how to spend a glorious day like this one. He stepped up beside her and took her hand. She looked at him curiously. What kind of boundaries was he expecting to have in their relationship?

He must have seen the question in her eyes because he asked, "Is it okay if I hold your hand?"

"I guess so, but I have to tell you, I'm very confused right now. I understand that you want a role in our baby's life, but what's this?" she asked, lifting up their combined hands.

"What it is will depend on you. Kate, knowing you has changed my life."

"Because of the baby. I get that. But I never meant to trap you with this pregnancy."

"I'm not talking about the baby right now. Just you. How do I put this?" He sighed. "It isn't easy."

They crossed the street and now Kate could see Central Park right in front of them. Miraculously, all the leaves seemed to be budding at the same time, smearing the trees with a vibrant light greenish glow—more a suggestion of color than the real thing.

"I used to think that I needed to run away from commitment in my life. I thought it was because I'd had too much of it, from a much too early age."

"And you had," she agreed.

"Maybe. But this weekend I realized that I was avoiding commitment in my relationships for another reason. Because I was afraid. Because I thought I would screw up. No matter how successful I became on the outside, inside I was still a loser."

She couldn't believe he would describe himself that way. "That is not you."

"But I didn't *believe* it. Not until I met you. When

I'm around you I feel like I have what it takes to be a good husband and a father…"

"Did you say *husband?*"

"…because I love you."

"Wait a minute—"

"Stop." He put a finger on her lips. "Before you say another word, I want you to know this. I'm offering you the whole package. It may be a bigger package than you expected, because Eric is part of the deal, but I love you and want to raise babies with you."

She could feel her eyes growing wider and her heart soared. But his finger was still on her mouth, and he wasn't finished talking.

"I never thought I wanted children, but if they're with you, nothing would make me happier."

Kate waited a few seconds before speaking. "You're done?"

"I'm done. You can shoot me down if you want. I just had to tell you how I feel."

"I can give you my answer now?"

He swallowed, then nodded.

Kate pulled her hands gently from his grasp and placed them on either side of his head. And then she kissed him.

The taste of Jay was something she'd never forgotten. The feel of his lips, the way his tongue probed against hers. Jay pulled her closer and returned her kiss like a man who'd been thinking of nothing but this for the past thirty-seven days.

Which happened to be the number of days since they'd last made love. And, yes, she'd been counting.

Finally he eased away. "I love kissing you. I could do it all night. But I want to know what you're thinking."

"That I love you. That I've never been happier. Even if it weren't for the baby, Jay, though of course I want this child very much."

He ran a hand over her hair, seeming to relish in just touching her. And she loved being touched by him. At the same time she needed him to understand what she was trying to say.

"I've missed you," he said. "Nothing has been as good without you. Especially at work."

"Would you consider going back to flying if we moved in together? That way Eric wouldn't be alone when you were out of town."

"Moving in together. I like the sound of that. And, hell yes, I'd love to get my old job back. Although I have an even better idea."

"Which is?"

"Will you marry me, Kate Cooper?"

"You're right. That is a *much* better idea."

He kissed her again, a long, slow, loving kiss. Then he made another proposition. "How about this? You and I get married. I go back to flying. And you fill in for me at Fox & Fisher. How does that sound?"

"Does the word *paradise* mean anything to you?"

Ever since she was a child, she'd longed to be part of a big, warm, loving family. Now her deepest wish was about to come true. Not just at work, where Lindsay, Nathan and Nadine were like the siblings she'd never had.

But at home, with Jay and Eric and the baby on its way, and the future babies, however many there might be.

The number no longer mattered. Because the important thing, above all else, was Jay.

* * * * *

*Be sure to look for C.J. Carmichael's next book
in March 2010, where Nadine takes on her very
own case and falls for the client in
RECEPTIONIST UNDER COVER!
Available wherever Harlequin books are sold.*

*Rancher Ramsey Westmoreland's temporary cook
is way too attractive for his liking.
Little does he know Chloe Burton came to his ranch
with another agenda entirely....*

That man across the street had to be, without a doubt, the most handsome man she'd ever seen.

Chloe Burton's pulse beat rhythmically as he stopped to talk to another man in front of a feed store. He was tall, dark and every inch of sexy—from his Stetson to the well-worn leather boots on his feet. And from the way his jeans and Western shirt fit his broad muscular shoulders, it was quite obvious he had everything it took to separate the men from the boys. The combination was enough to corrupt any woman's mind and had her weakening even from a distance. Her body felt flushed. It was hot. Unsettled.

Over the past year the only male who had gotten her time and attention had been the e-mail. That was simply pathetic, especially since now she was practically drooling simply at the sight of a man. Even his stance—both hands in his jeans pockets, legs braced apart, was a pose she would carry to her dreams.

And he was smiling, evidently enjoying the conversation being exchanged. He had dimples, incredibly sexy dimples in not one but both cheeks.

"What are you staring at, Clo?"

Chloe nearly jumped. She'd forgotten she had a lunch date. She glanced over the table at her best friend from college, Lucia Conyers.

"Take a look at that man across the street in the blue shirt, Lucia. Will he not be perfect for Denver's first issue of *Simply Irresistible* or what?" Chloe asked with so much excitement she almost couldn't stand it.

She was the owner of *Simply Irresistible*, a magazine for today's up-and-coming woman. Their once-a-year Irresistible Man cover, which highlighted a man the magazine felt deserved the honor, had increased sales enough for Chloe to open a Denver office.

When Lucia didn't say anything but kept staring, Chloe's smile widened. "Well?"

Lucia glanced across the booth at her. "Since you asked, I'll tell you what I see. One of the Westmorelands—Ramsey Westmoreland. And yes, he'd be perfect for the cover, but he won't do it."

Chloe raised a brow. "He'd get paid for his services, of course."

Lucia laughed and shook her head. "Getting paid won't be the issue, Clo—Ramsey is one of the wealthiest sheep ranchers in this part of Colorado. But everyone knows what a private person he is. Trust me—he won't do it."

Chloe couldn't help but smile. The man was the epitome of what she was looking for in a magazine cover and she was determined that whatever it took, he would be it.

"Umm, I don't like that look on your face, Chloe. I've seen it before and know exactly what it means."

She watched as Ramsey Westmoreland entered the store with a swagger that made her almost breathless. She *would* be seeing him again.

Look for Silhouette Desire's
HOT WESTMORELAND NIGHTS
by Brenda Jackson,
available March 9 wherever books are sold.

Devastating, dark-hearted and...
looking for brides.

Look for

BOUGHT:
DESTITUTE YET DEFIANT
by *Sarah Morgan*
#2902

From the lowliest slums to Millionaire's Row...
these men have everything now but their brides—
and they'll settle for nothing less than the best!

Available March 2010
from Harlequin Presents!

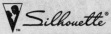

ROMANTIC
SUSPENSE

Sparked by Danger, Fueled by Passion.

Introducing a brand-new miniseries
Lawmen of Black Rock

Peyton Wilkerson's life shatters when her
four-month-old daughter, Lilly, vanishes.
But handsome sheriff Tom Grayson is
determined to put the pieces together and
reunite her with her baby. Will Tom be able
to protect Peyton and Lilly while fighting
his own growing feelings?

Find out in
His Case, Her Baby
by
CARLA CASSIDY

Available in March wherever books are sold

REQUEST YOUR FREE BOOKS!

2 FREE NOVELS PLUS 2 FREE GIFTS!

HARLEQUIN®

Super Romance®

Exciting, emotional, unexpected!

YES! Please send me 2 FREE Harlequin® Superromance® novels and my 2 FREE gifts (gifts are worth about $10). After receiving them, if I don't wish to receive any more books, I can return the shipping statement marked "cancel." If I don't cancel, I will receive 6 brand-new novels every month and be billed just $4.69 per book in the U.S. or $5.24 per book in Canada. That's a saving of close to 15% off the cover price! It's quite a bargain! Shipping and handling is just 50¢ per book in the U.S. and 75¢ per book in Canada.* I understand that accepting the 2 free books and gifts places me under no obligation to buy anything. I can always return a shipment and cancel at any time. Even if I never buy another book from Harlequin, the two free books and gifts are mine to keep forever.

135 HDN E4JC   336 HDN E4JN

Name _____ (PLEASE PRINT)

Address _____ Apt. #

City _____ State/Prov. _____ Zip/Postal Code

Signature (if under 18, a parent or guardian must sign)

Mail to the **Harlequin Reader Service:**
IN U.S.A.: P.O. Box 1867, Buffalo, NY 14240-1867
IN CANADA: P.O. Box 609, Fort Erie, Ontario L2A 5X3

Not valid for current subscribers to Harlequin Superromance books.

**Are you a current subscriber to Harlequin Superromance books
and want to receive the larger-print edition?
Call 1-800-873-8635 today!**

* Terms and prices subject to change without notice. Prices do not include applicable taxes. N.Y. residents add applicable sales tax. Canadian residents will be charged applicable provincial taxes and GST. Offer not valid in Quebec. This offer is limited to one order per household. All orders subject to approval. Credit or debit balances in a customer's account(s) may be offset by any other outstanding balance owed by or to the customer. Please allow 4 to 6 weeks for delivery. Offer available while quantities last.

Your Privacy: Harlequin Books is committed to protecting your privacy. Our Privacy Policy is available online at www.eHarlequin.com or upon request from the Reader Service. From time to time we make our lists of customers available to reputable third parties who may have a product or service of interest to you. If you would prefer we not share your name and address, please check here. ☐

Help us get it right—We strive for accurate, respectful and relevant communications. To clarify or modify your communication preferences, visit us at www.ReaderService.com/consumerchoice.

HSR10

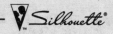

SPECIAL EDITION

FROM *USA TODAY* BESTSELLING AUTHOR
CHRISTINE RIMMER

BRAVO FAMILY TIES

A BRIDE FOR
JERICHO BRAVO

Marnie Jones had long ago buried her wild-child
impulses and opted to be "safe," romantically
speaking. But one look at born rebel Jericho Bravo
and she began to wonder if her thrill-seeking side
was about to be revived. Because if ever there was
a man worth taking a chance on, there he was,
right within her grasp....

*Available in March
wherever books are sold.*

Visit Silhouette Books at www.eHarlequin.com

SSE65511